# Other books by Nancy Lynn Jarvis

Mags and the AARP Gang
The Truth About Hosting Airbnb

## Regan McHenry Real Estate Mysteries
The Death Contingency
Backyard Bones
Buying Murder
The Widow's Walk League
The Murder House
A Neighborly Killing
The Two-Faced Triplex

## PIP Inc. Mysteries
The Funeral Murder

## Edited books
Cozy Food: 128 Cozy Mystery Writers Share Their Favorite Recipes

Santa Cruz Weird

# The Glass House

## A PIP Inc. Mystery

# Nancy Lynn Jarvis

Good Read Mysteries
An imprint of Good Read Publishers

*Happy reading, Sylvia*

*Nancy Lynn Jarvis*

This is a work of fiction. Unless specifically credited, names, characters, places, and incidents are either products of the author's imagination or are used fictitiously.
Any resemblance to actual events, locales, or persons, living or dead, is entirely coincidental.

**Good Read
Mysteries**

Good Read Mysteries © is a registered trademark of Good Read Publishers
301 Azalea Lane, Santa Cruz, California, 95060

Copyright ©July 2019 by Nancy Kille

Library of Congress Control Number: 2019940650
ISBN Number: 9780997366754

Printed in the United States of America

www.nancylynnjarvis.com

Books are available at special quantity discounts through the website.

"… unrequited love does not die; it's only beaten down to a secret place where it hides, curled and wounded. For some unfortunates, it turns bitter and mean, and those who come after pay the price for the hurt done by the one who came before." —Elle Newmark

# Acknowledgments

Thanks to my friend Pat Pfremmer, the real private investigator Pat, for her stories and for letting me use her as the inspiration for Pat Pirard in PIP Inc.

Thanks to glass artist Jan Tozzo, owner of Glass Pieces, who inspired this story, and to Laurie Spray, one of Jan's teachers, for letting me borrow her studio for location.

Thanks, too, to renowned glass artist Craig Mitchell Smith, for suggesting how to commit murder.

Editing by Morgan Rankin and by Elizabeth Brown
www.SwiftEdits.com

Cover design by Jessica Tahbonemah and Jenn Wright.

# The Glass House

## A PIP Inc. Mystery

Nancy Lynn Jarvis

"R-E-S," Pat belted out letters with Aretha, "P-E-C-T" as she pulled into the parking spot labeled "Law Librarian" at the Santa Cruz County Building. There weren't enough employee spaces for everyone who worked in the multistory building, so getting a designated spot just before her thirty-fifth birthday was a serious coup. Pat turned off her car's engine, suspending Aretha's anthem in mid-note.

Such a special parking space warranted a special car, and as of a week ago Thursday, Pat owned precisely the right one to fill it. She had turned in her ancient practical Honda and treated herself to a sunburst-yellow Mercedes two-door coupe, a gift to herself for her milestone birthday. The car wasn't new, but it was perfect—distinctive and her favorite color—and since she had managed to save the $27,000 it cost, she had a pink slip to go with it. Never mind that her savings account read zero, her ride was worth becoming destitute.

She flipped the sunscreen flap down to reveal a mirror, checked her strawberry blonde hair for strays, and made sure her peachy lipstick didn't need a touch-up. Satisfied, she flipped the sunshield back up against the car's ceiling and opened the car door. Pat's stylish pointed-toe pumps hit the pavement and she slid out of her car, tugging her leopard-print briefcase with her.

She felt life was, if not perfect, at least good, better than it was a few months ago and getting better every day. The parking space and her car helped, but her attitude was hard won after her recent history. It was good she had made so much progress because as she went to work, she had no idea how different her life was going to be by the end of the day, let alone by the end of the month.

It had been eight months since she caught Rick, her long-term boyfriend, kissing "an old friend" he ran into unexpectedly, and almost six months since he had asked her to join him at their favorite romantic date-night restaurant. He said he had something important to ask her. She expected a proposal. What she got was a confession that the old friend was a former girlfriend and that she and Rick had rekindled their relationship. The important question Rick had to ask was her forgiveness for stringing her along while he explored his feelings for his old flame.

She had wished him—them—well. It was a classy thing to do, but she didn't mean a word of it.

Pat's best friend, Syda, was the sort of woman who favored getting on the next horse out of the stable to recover from a fall, so when Pat called her with her heartbreaking news, she had bounded into action. She had given Pat one week, a carton of mocha fudge ice cream, and as many tears as she could fit into that time frame before she started pushing masculine finds in Pat's direction. Each came with the promise that they were a perfect match for a nice rebound romance.

First up had been Syda's yoga instructor. "He's single, straight, and gorgeous. Wait till you see his biceps. They'll make you forget all about that cheating Rick," Syda had promised. "And he's so dedicated to his students; you'll be impressed."

Pat had made a face like a first grader might make when her mother told her she had to wear her new sensible navy blue rain boots because last year's ladybug boots didn't fit her any longer. But Pat had borrowed a yoga mat from Syda, put on cute yoga pants, and allowed herself to be dragged to class. Reluctantly.

"What have you got to lose?" Syda had quizzed on the drive. "Even if you don't like him, you'll get your exercise done for the day."

To any mildly observant person, and Pat was considerably above average when it came to observation, it was obvious the dedicated yoga instructor taught the class in large part because it put him in front of an admiring and ardent—and Pat wagered occasionally pliant—audience, which he could leisurely assess from behind as his students worked on their downward dog.

As it turned out, Pat was not impressed.

Syda's second choice for Pat's get-back-in-the-game romance had been the assistant manager of a small trendy food store. Syda had taken Pat shopping and arranged an accidental meeting between her and the assistant manager in the produce department. He was mildly attractive, and Pat loved vegetables. The meeting held some promise until Syda had decided to hurry things along.

"Could you tell us how to pick the best dragon fruit?" Syda asked. "My friend, Pat, who is single, by the way, wants to know if you should squeeze it hard, or just softly." Syda tittered suggestively.

The assistant manager had turned the color of one of the plump beets stacked in a nearby bin.

Pat had been mortified.

Pat spied him four days after their encounter, not in front of his store, which she was assiduously avoiding for the time being, but in the Safeway parking lot. He was wrangling three grade-school kids into his car, screaming at them the entire time.

Any thought she might have had about a return visit to New Leaf Market—sans Syda—for exotic fruits and vegetables vanished immediately. She knew she didn't need that kind of drama in her life; besides, she didn't like men who yelled at kids.

Syda was disappointed. "You're going to wind up alone," she warned her friend.

"Right now that sounds good," Pat fired back. "A rebound romance doesn't appeal to me."

Syda backed off and let Pat have some space and time, but she couldn't resist playing matchmaker forever. Syda's next scheme had been presented the day before Pat bought her new car.

"Come over to dinner next week—you pick the day—

but give me a couple of days' warning." Syda thought her invitation had been presented so casually that Pat would never guess she had an ulterior motive.

Pat smelled another set-up. "Why do you need to know in advance?" she asked, trying to entrap Syda. "Usually you invite me over the same day you want to see me."

"Umm," Syda had rolled her eyes looking for an explanation, "because Greg volunteered for the swing shift for the next two weeks, and I want to make sure he arranges his schedule so he can join us?" Syda's voice rose by the time she reached the end of what should have been a statement. She hadn't seemed to notice, though, and she had smiled broadly. Too broadly, Pat noted, to look sincere.

"Oh," Syda had added, attempting to act like her request was an off-handed afterthought, "and you might want to wear your green dress."

"My green dress? The one with the plunging neckline? Just for you and Greg?" a mischievous Pat had asked.

"Well, if Greg rearranges shifts, it may mean trading hours with another team, and he may have to bring a fellow officer along. Greg's on temporary assignment with an officer whose partner is on vacation like his is. He's pretty happy about the arrangement because he partnered with the guy when he was new to the Santa Cruz Sheriff's Department. They've remained friendly. So your green dress might not just be for us."

"What does Greg think about your little dinner plan?"

"Oh, he's the one who thought you should meet his

friend. I don't know him exactly; I've only met him in passing, but…" Syda had thrown her hand over her mouth when she realized how much she had said and how badly she had blown her cover story.

Syda's meet-up track record may have been abysmal, but Greg's was untested. In his line of work, Greg had to make quick decisions about people or he could wind up dead. She trusted his people-reading skills much more than her well-intentioned, but desperate-to-play-matchmaker buddy's. Greg was a good guy, too, and likely to be friendly with others who shared his standards. He knew Pat well and cared about her almost as much as his wife did. He also had a bit of a knight-helping-a-damsel-in-distress temperament so, even though Pat had never considered herself in need of rescuing, she knew Greg's heart was always in the right place.

Most importantly, though, Greg had never been that fond of Rick—and wasn't shy about saying so. He got that right, as it turned out, so if Greg thought she and his friend should meet, Pat was sort of willing to accept the dinner invitation. Soon.

"Okay, Syda," Pat had acquiesced, "but not next week. I know you're trying to help…"

"Well, of course I am. That's what best friends do."

"…but I'm fine, Syda. I have a job I love, a cute little house to rent, my dog and cat, and I'm about to treat myself to the car of my dreams. Don't worry about me. I don't need a man in my life to be happy."

"I know that, but it's just that I want everything for

you." Syda had spread her hands palms up in explanation.

Pat had grabbed her and given her a hug. "Let me get past my birthday and have a little more time without you trying to fix me up and then, well, we'll see. Full disclosure, though, when I come to dinner, I'm not wearing my green dress."

She bought her car two days later and was contented, even if Syda didn't think so.

Pat turned for one last glance at her gleaming sunshine-yellow car and then walked down the ramp to the lower level of the County Building where the Law Library was housed. As she approached the doorway, the sensor clanked the door open. As usual, she startled at the sound. As many times as she came in this way and as many times as the door had opened for her, the sound it made was always awe-inspiring: castle gates with rusty hinges being parted by armored cavaliers ready to do battle with invaders. It closed behind her with the same flourish.

Pat walked down the long, empty corridor, her high heels clacking on the concrete floor. Some people might have found the entry to the Law Library off-putting. Overhead florescent lights shone too brightly and cast an obviously artificial glow. Pipes strung overhead reminded her that she was in a subterranean place. But the ceiling was high, and she knew the County Building basement was overbuilt and ready to become ground control in the event of an earthquake or other natural disaster. The setting made her feel secure, nestled, and protected.

Halfway down the hall a bump-in with high glass doors announced the Santa Cruz County Law Library in black and gold lettering. Pat pushed the door open—it creaked, too, but nothing like the building's entry door—and let herself into the paneled coziness that was the Law Library.

"Hi, Jefferson," she greeted the assistant law librarian who was just taking his seat behind the intake counter. "Any interesting questions from attorneys that need immediate researching?"

"Not really, Pat. I left one note on your desk, but he said, 'no rush,' and your phone's been quiet so far this morning." Jefferson busied himself with making sure his showy bow tie was straight. "Oh, but Dick Drinker called. He wants to come by right before we close at noon. He wanted to know if you preferred chocolate or lemon. I told him lemon. Was that a good call?"

It was Friday, the day before her birthday. Pat was sure the lemon/chocolate question was about cake flavors. She had a great relationship with Dick Drinker, the Library Board president, and she would have bet her new car he was going to stop by with some of the other attorneys she helped on a regular basis to sing "Happy Birthday" and present her with a cake.

"You can't go wrong with either chocolate or lemon cake, Jefferson," she smiled. "Great tie."

Pat poked her head into each of the three rooms of stacks which housed over 16,000 massive leather-bound volumes of the law, checking for legals or members of the public who might need assistance before entering her small office, but she and Jefferson were the only ones in the Law Library.

She was happy to have some alone time to enjoy her office. It was fronted with a large window so she could see what was happening in her domain, although the stacks with their books and tables for spreading out while researching were hidden from her view. Originally it came equipped with a standard-issue metal desk, table, and filing cabinets, and an ergonomically correct and functional rolling chair. The walls held pictures of several prominent judges evenly spaced out around the room, all hung a little too high for the average person viewing the photos to meet their gaze. She asked if she could paint the muted white walls a bright color, since there were no exterior windows and no natural light, but was told she couldn't. It seemed a work-around was in order.

Once she was officially given the title of Law Librarian four-and-a-half-years ago and her weekend key was bestowed, she went to work on the office to make it hers. Pat changed all the lightbulbs to full-spectrum daylight, which helped tremendously. Next she returned the desk and file cabinets to county storage and had some friends help her bring in her inherited grandfather's mahogany desk. It was massive and much too big for her rental house, but it was just right at center stage in her new office.

She purchased metal filing cabinets off Craigslist and spray-painted them in rainbow hues. She duplicitously explained the colors helped her keep her work organized better, but the truth was that she liked their bright disruption of an otherwise staid environment.

The judges were the next thing she tackled. They got moved and massed on the two end walls of her office. She formed tidy squares with them, each three pictures high and three pictures wide, nine judges per square, just like the number of justices in the Supreme Court. They were visually more accessible in their new locations, and she imagined they enjoyed their proximity.

Her rearranging left the wall behind her desk, the largest wall in her office by far, bare. She remedied that with one of Syda's paintings: a huge decent-if-not-perfect rendition of Santa Cruz's surfer statue done in a foreshortened panorama so some blue water from Monterey Bay and the Santa Cruz Lighthouse could be squeezed into the scene. Her office was unconventional for a law librarian's, but then she was an unconventional law librarian, and since she was so good at her job, no one minded her improvements.

Pat settled into her seat, plopped her briefcase on her desk, and snapped it open. She reached inside for the two pieces of research she'd taken home with her last night and put them on her desk before putting her briefcase and purse into one of her grandfather's enormous desk drawers. She dialed the number neatly written on the sticky tab on page one of the first report.

"Law offices," a professional, well-modulated voice greeted her.

"Hello, Mark Bellows, please."

"Just a moment."

"Mark Bellows," a deep, friendly voice answered.

"Hi, Mark, it's Pat Pirard. I have the reference you need for your Carson case."

"Thanks, Pat, I'll stop by a little before noon and we can go over it then."

Pat liked the idea of seeing Mark in person. He was tall, bright, good-looking, with a sprinkling of premature gray in his hair that made him look distinguished, and recently divorced. His visits to the Law Library had become more frequent since his marriage ended, and she thought even more frequent after Jefferson mentioned her breakup to one of his firm's paralegals. Gossip in the law community was currency, just like it was in any other bureaucracy, and Jefferson had traded some juicy info about Pat over lunch with a young woman as he tried to convince her to give him first pick from her Jack Russell terrier's litter of pups. No doubt she mentioned Pat's breakup to others, and within a few days, everyone knew Rick was no more.

Pat absentmindedly tucked a strand of hair behind her ear and, when she realized what she had done, chuckled out loud. Syda would be pleased to know that Pat was exhibiting behavior widely recognized as interest in and encouragement of the opposite sex.

She turned to the final information request and dialed the number on its sticky note. A very different greeter answered.

"You have reached the law office of Roger Drago and Associates. How may I direct your call?" a woman with a strong New Jersey accent asked.

In her mind, Pat put the woman in a noir movie and saw the receptionist leaning back in her seat with the phone tucked under her chin while she inspected a fingernail that was losing its bright red polish at the tip. Pat knew Roger Drago was a one-man law firm and that his receptionist was his sister, but she played along.

"Mr. Drago, please."

"Drago here."

"Hi, Roger, it's Pat Pirard. I've finished researching that question you had for me."

"You're a doll. Mind if I swing by a little before noon so we can yammer about it?"

"That would be fine, Roger."

Pat smiled as she hung up. It seemed pretty clear to her that cake and attorneys singing was on her day's schedule. With luck, her cake would be a lemon sponge with Meyer lemon curd filling and chocolate ganache frosting from The Buttery.

Her day went by quickly and, as Pat predicted, ended with a parade of attorneys and their staff marching into the Law Library at 11:45 singing "Happy Birthday." Mark Bellows motioned her out of her office into the much larger reception area while the song progressed, because there were too many well-wishers to fit in her office.

Also, as she predicted, Dick Drinker carried a sheet cake frosted with chocolate ganache and prickled with thirty-five candles. He sat it on the reception counter and began lighting the candles. It took more than one match to get them all going, and for just a moment, that need made Pat feel like the first phase of her life, the one with youth and goals and the promise that anything was possible, was about to end. But the feeling passed and it wasn't until Dick Drinker, president of the Library Board of Trustees, ushered her back into her office after everyone left that she discovered how right her hunch had been.

"Thank you so much for the cake and organizing the happy birthday singing party. There were so many people; I'm overwhelmed. You were the one who did that, weren't you?" Pat glowed with the honor she had just received and from eating a large piece of Buttery cake.

"I was. Pat, we need to talk," Dick started out simply enough.

For someone she had just thanked for making her so happy, Pat thought Dick looked quite morose. She tilted her head just a bit and asked evenly, "What do we need to talk about, exactly?"

"I think you should take a seat." He motioned her to her chair and perched awkwardly on the edge of the county-issued metal table. He leaned toward her like a sage father about to have a heart-to-heart with his daughter.

"You know how we all respect you and appreciate the work you do for us. You just saw how much we all love you, too, which makes this so much harder. The Law Library is funded from legal fees and donations from the legal community, and while I'm the president of the Library Board of Trustees, I have much less to say about how this place gets run than you might think."

Pat listened carefully. Dick wasn't telling her anything she didn't already know, and it was concerning that he seemed to need a preamble like he had just given for whatever it was he was about to say.

"The thing is, court filing fees are down and there's been a lot of pressure on the Law Library budget, and that's not even counting the employee pension situation that's barely begun to rear its ugly head. There have been calls to save money any way possible."

Pat spoke quickly to defend her beloved institution. "The Law Library is mandated. It can't be cut."

"No, it can't, but budgetary cuts are still required. The Board of Trustees decided the size of our Law Library doesn't warrant a law librarian and an assistant law librarian."

Pat felt a momentary pity-pang for Jefferson until she realized where Dick's speech was going.

"Jefferson makes half of what you do, Pat, and while he won't be as good as you are initially, maybe—probably—he'll never be as good as you are—you've trained him well. He'll suffice."

Pat understood how it must have felt to the French Revolutionaries who were deemed by the next wave to have been too lenient, and were shown to Madame la Guillotine for their sympathy.

"You're firing me?"

"Not firing. Of course, not firing. Firing implies that you did something wrong. You're being downsized."

"Semantics aside, I'm being let go?"

"I'm afraid so. I did everything I could, but the Trustees' vote was four to one. I did get you a good severance package: six weeks. And you have a week's vacation remaining and sick days. I arranged that you could be sick for the next ten days and have your package start after that."

Pat swallowed repeatedly, trying not to be woozy. "You aren't wrong about the sick days. Right now I feel quite ill."

Dick's distress was genuine. "I'm so sorry, Pat."

Pat stiffened her back. "May I keep my key for a few days? I'll get my things out by…" She had to stop speaking and compose herself. "I have to make arrangements for some help; I'll get my things out by Wednesday."

"No, Pat. The least I can do is hire someone to get your desk and file cabinets moved. Shall I have them delivered to your house?"

She nodded silently. Pat opened the desk drawer where she had put her briefcase and her purse. She detached her after-hours key from her key ring and handed it to Dick Drinker. "Don't forget my painting. I'd take it now but it won't fit in my car."

He walked her out. Pat startled one last time as the outside doors boomed and creaked open and closed, rendering her forever an outsider. She got into her car, closed the door, gave him a little wave, and waited until he had gone before she leaned her head against the steering wheel and sobbed.

❋❋❋❋❋❋❋❋❋❋

Saturday's weather was as she hoped it would be in late May: sunny and not yet into the summer pattern that brought fog to Santa Cruz in June, July, and August. She had decided on a low-key themed backyard birthday party—which she had dubbed a Treinta y Cinco de Mayo party on her invitations—that began in the late afternoon.

In keeping with her theme, guests would enjoy do-it-yourself tacos built using corn or flour tortillas. Tacos, with their varied fillings, were perfect foils for the gluten free, vegans, vegetarians, and carnivores among her friends. Pitchers of strawberry margaritas and Dos Equis beers were in the fridge chilling, and a multilayered, multicolored birthday cake was ready to be served.

Pat had scored a piñata in Watsonville where they were always available if you went to the right Mexican *supermacado*, but so soon after Cinco de Mayo, she had many choices and picked a huge star with dangling point streamers. She had hired a small mariachi band to stop by around 5:30. They were to leave by 7:30 in consideration of her neighbors who might not appreciate such raucous music.

Her planning skills were excellent so everything was under control and ready for her birthday party by midday. The only problem was Pat's mood; it wasn't as good as she expected, but then, she hadn't expected to be fired the day before her big day.

At 3:00 she was putting on fresh lipstick and checking her hair, trying to decide if the red hibiscus she stole from a table decoration would look better pinned above her right or left ear, and giving herself a pep talk via her Dalmatian who was sitting at attention watching her process. She spoke in the direction of her bathroom mirror, but her words and reflected gaze were directed toward her dog.

"I have acting skills, you know. I minored in theater arts in college. I can smile all day long like I mean it. Besides, I probably won't have to fake being cheery for long; I'll probably forget all about yesterday once people start arriving. Don't you think I'm right, Dot?"

Dot seemed to smile back in concurrence—Dalmatians were noted for being some of the best smilers in the dog world—and Pat gained confidence from her pet's agreement.

She would have asked her cat's opinion, too, but Wimsey had witnessed party prep, decided something that would interfere with his relaxed sunbathing was afoot, and abandoned Pat's backyard for a sunny spot in the next-door neighbor's yard where his cat buddy, Thomas, lived.

Party prep was going perfectly until her office remains arrived at 3:15.

"Where do you want this stuff?" mover number one asked when she answered his clamorous knock on her front door. "I figure you don't want me leaving it on the sidewalk. Nice flower," he nodded toward the hibiscus above her left ear.

"Now? You're bringing my furniture and Syda's

17

painting now?"

"You're very observant. Yes, it appears me and my helper are bringing your stuff now. Inside or outside?" he asked unsympathetically.

"Inside. In the spare bedroom. I haven't had a chance to organize it for the desk…"

"Perfect. We'll leave the desk just inside your spare bedroom door and you can play with your spatial arrangements at your leisure."

Mover number one turned his head away from Pat and yelled to his partner, "Yo, Jimmy, we got another big-desk-small-door situation here, so we gotta' take out the drawers and turn it sideways."

Mover number two groaned and rolled his eyes as he started removing drawers.

"Save the desk for last. Let's bring in the classy rainbow filing cabinets and the big objet d'art first."

Pat tried to shut the spare bedroom door after the movers left, but the desk blocked the door enough that she couldn't close it. She propped Syda's Santa Cruz surfer painting in front of it and hoped anyone who noticed it would think it was all part of her party decorations and not ask her any questions about why her guest room was full to overflowing with office furniture.

Her plan worked until Syda and Greg arrived and Syda caught a glimpse of her painting.

"Hey, Birthday Girl, shouldn't my painting be at the Law Library?"

"Come have a margarita and ask me that question after

the party's over, okay?"

Pat circulated and hosted and her guests had a good time, but she found herself acting the entire day. She was exhausted by the time the party ended. Greg was taking out the trash and Pat had run out of diversionary tactics by the time she and Syda were loading the dishwasher.

"So, what's the backstory with my painting?" Syda asked. "Are you tired of it? I know it's not my best work, but I think it's interesting. Why is it in your guest room? Spill."

"Because I'm thirty-five and unemployed."

"What do you mean, 'unemployed'?"

"Did you notice that my good friend, Dick Drinker, was conspicuously absent from the festivities today? I invited him and his wife, but I guess he couldn't face me after firing me yesterday," Pat said as she emptied the dregs of the pitcher of margaritas into a glass, downed it, and then tried to squeeze the now-empty container into the dishwasher.

"He fired you?" Syda's eyebrows disappeared under her bangs. "They love you at the Law Library. He can't fire you."

"Dick Drinker used the politer term 'downsized' when he told me I was fired. I've got nine weeks to get myself a new source of income before I run out of money. Will you and Greg let me use your couch if I become homeless?"

"Mi coucha es tu coucha," Greg said as he returned from dump-run duty. "I missed the start. Why will you be couch surfing at our house?"

19

"Pat's been let go by the Law Library. Imagine!" Syda's voice held outrage.

"I hope you did something scandalous to get fired," Greg laughed.

"This is serious," Syda oozed sympathy.

"I got to be too expensive for them. The assistant law librarian has been elevated in title but not pay. I noticed Jefferson wasn't here today, either. Cowards all," Pat harrumphed.

"I'm sure something will turn up," Greg reassured. "You can apply in the Santa Cruz County Library system. They'll have an opening, won't they?"

"I'm a law librarian. I do legal research. I work with law books and databases. I don't know the first thing about bestsellers or children's books, and I'm not sure I want to learn about them. I like solving puzzles and looking for esoteric answers."

"So what you're saying is that you're a snob librarian," Greg teased.

"Don't pay any attention to him. What you need is to give yourself a few days off. You need a diversion, and I know just the thing. I'm starting a glass class on Tuesday. It's taught by a world-renowned glass artist—a master peony designer—and even though the class is full, I'm sure I can call in a favor and get you into it. Leave everything to me," Syda beamed. "You can't turn me down. The class is my birthday present to you."

"Ahh, my wife is never happier than when she's making plans for someone's life, especially when that someone doesn't need their life planned, but you know she's going to hound you until you agree. And she's right. Take a couple of days to clear your head before you start a job search. Nine weeks is a long time and, if need be, we have a very comfortable couch."

Like it or not, on Tuesday morning Pat found herself in Syda's van on her way up Bonny Doon Road into the redwood forest.

"This is going to be so much fun," Syda gushed. "I've been looking for my medium and I think glass is going to be it. Who knows, maybe we'll both excel at glass art, form a team and our own business, and become famous like Annieglass. She started out small and now she manufactures in Watsonville and ships worldwide. She employs a bunch of people; we could be CEOs, as well as artists."

Pat listened silently as Syda planned their future—there was no point in trying to interrupt her when she was rolling—and told her what her immediate future held.

"The teacher is Garryn Monteith. He's a creative genius. He has his own galley in New York, displays in museums, and sells to rich Arab families. We are so lucky, honored really, to have him here."

"Why is he here? If he's so renowned, why does he want to teach a little class in Santa Cruz?"

"That's the best part about him. He likes to give back to the art community. He takes time out of his incredibly demanding schedule to come here a couple of times a year.

He says he enjoys the one-on-one with students. And I've heard that he and Lillian Wentner, the woman who owns the glass studio where we're going and who is pretty famous in her own right—she sells well in Carmel galleries—go way back. I think he does it as a favor for her. He splits his class fees with her so she makes some serious money hosting him.

"He does lots of other things, too, but he's famous for making these amazing wild peonies. Did you know wild peonies come in many colors, everything from lavender to white to yellow to pink? You get to pick the color you want to make. I'm going to use lavender glass. I love lavender, it's so soothing and healing."

"Are you sure those qualities translate to glass? I thought it was the scent that was soothing."

"Well maybe, but I love the color, too. What color will you choose?"

Pat shrugged. "Yellow?"

"What's the address for the Glass House?" Syda asked. "Oh, never mind. I see the welcome banner." She turned her van into the driveway, through the prettily manicured surroundings, past the two-story farmhouse which was outlined with a huge bed of flowers, some real and some made out of glass propped up on various lengths of metal stems, to the back of the property where other cars were parked in front of a long wooden building with a high-pitched roof and an L-shaped extension.

"We're supposed to meet at the main house," Syda said as she parked.

23

Pat trailed Syda to the house, where they found a door which was slightly ajar. Syda pushed it open and leaned her head forward to peer inside.

"Don't be shy, come on in," a friendly masculine voice invited. "We have scones right out of the oven, and coffee."

Pat was greeted by a fabulous aroma. She recognized the scent of spices—cinnamon and a hint of cardamom—emanating from the linen-lined basket filled with perfectly browned scones, which were strong enough to compete with the smell of fresh-brewed coffee. The tall middle-aged man with a slightly receding hairline who had shouted out greetings stood behind the counter where the scones and coffee were.

"Oooh," Syda intoned as she rushed to take him up on his offer. Scone in one hand and a cup of coffee in the other, she moved toward a group of women at the far side of the kitchen where a fireplace stood.

Pat picked up a cup of coffee as she asked him, "Are you the creative genius my friend was telling me about on the ride here?"

He produced a broad smile. "I did make the scones and coffee. Does that qualify me for that designation?"

"The coffee does," Pat replied after she took a sip.

"I think your friend was talking about the guy in the knot of adoring females over there. He's Garryn Monteith, visiting sensation."

"I'm Pat, not one of his acolytes." She switched her coffee to her left hand and held out her freed right hand for a handshake.

"I'm just Joe, Joe Wentner, chief cook and bottle washer at this event. I'm Lillian Wentner's husband. I have no artistic talent, so I'll be in charge of lunch."

"You bake and make the best coffee I've ever had. That's having artistic talent, as far as I'm concerned. I hope your wife appreciates what you do."

He didn't answer. Instead he raised his eyebrows, tilted his head, and raised his shoulders slightly in a gesture that said he wondered.

The gaggle of women on the far side of the kitchen collectively took a step back to reveal a man at its center. He was of slightly less-than-average height, although he tried to appear taller by wearing a gelled, carefully coiffed, spiked hairdo. His looks were ordinary except for his smile, which showed a row of very even, glowingly white upper teeth as well as part of his lower teeth. It was a practiced smile, Pat thought, but one that had been practiced for so long that it had become internalized and no longer looked forced. His hand movement as he bade them follow him was slightly theatrical, as was his language and its delivery.

"Come, my darlings, it's time we begin our journey of learning and artistic endeavor."

He stepped forward, and though he was dressed unceremoniously in kakis and a blue pinstriped shirt rolled to his elbows, he moved as if he wore a golden crown and had on a floor-length cape that fluttered behind him. He definitely had that attribute which was impossible to explain, but was recognizable when it was seen: he had star quality. He held his arm out to Lillian Wentner, who took it like his queen. The procession that followed him out the kitchen door was, with just a couple of exceptions, filled with adoring, puppy-dog-eyed women. Pat noted Syda was among them.

"Come on, come on," she said as she hooked her arm through Pat's and dragged her forward. Pat reluctantly returned her half-full coffee cup to the counter before she was swept out the door.

"Show of hands, please," Garryn Monteith asked once the women were settled at their stations around a bay of three worktables that took up most of the long part of the building. "How many of you are virgins?"

The audience erupted with tittering.

"Never fear. I'm here to help you lose your virginity."

There was more laughter.

"I'm talking about glass-crafting virgins, of course. Oh, you naughty girls. What did you think I meant?" He guffawed and smiled, showing more teeth than Pat thought could fit in one person's mouth.

"I want you all to go to the glass sheet bin and pick out a big piece of your favorite color and some complementary colors for petals. You'll all need some bright yellow as well. Today we'll learn how to cut and arrange petals and prep them for the kiln. Then we'll go to work on the spiders. Oh, don't go squeamish on me. The glass stamens, which are the trickiest part, will look like spiders after the first firing. We'll fire the stamens and flat petals tonight so we get melting and blending of colors for a realistic look and make the stamens. Tomorrow we'll drape the flat petals until they form gorgeous natural-looking flowers. I have the most amazing ideas for you on what to use to make them shape beautifully, and then the third day…"

Pat expected him to say, "I'll rise from the dead," given how the women in his class seemed to worship him and how he seemed to feel about himself.

"…we'll make any necessary tweaks to your work—although with me as your instructor, I expect all your flowers will be perfect—and I'll share my secret method for attaching everything to stems so you can display them using my patented stem system. And then we'll drink wine and celebrate." He finished with an upsurge to his voice and his hands raised and swirling in the air.

Pat scanned the room as Garryn Monteith spoke. Most of the students, including Syda and even his co-teacher Lillian Wentner, looked at him with mesmerized half-smiles on their faces. She did note three women who, like her, were not part of his adoring pack. Those women were the ones she wanted to spend time with during the lunch break.

Glass cutting was fairly straightforward, but Pat had to admit her teacher did offer tips that helped the process. She also had to admit that his nonstop stories were entertaining. She couldn't help but enjoy them and, his ego aside, she found herself reluctantly warming to him because of his skill as instructor and storyteller. By lunchtime she had completed her petals. She had decided on sunny yellow as the primary petal color and chose a creamy off-white for a complementary color.

Garryn Monteith, spouting stories as he moved, began the morning walking up and down the tables offering personal words for his students. "You are going to be one of my star pupils, Pat. Your eye for color is fabulous," Garryn Monteith raved. "Your petals will have so much depth and realism because of your choices."

When Garryn Monteith made his second round of the tables, Syda was still in deep concentration mode, her focus only interrupted by an occasional swearword when she failed to get exactly the shape she wanted. He passed over her with a simple, "I'd snip a bit there," as encouragement and moved to hover over Pat.

He threw a fingertip kiss to her, a kiss Pat thought more appropriately might have been delivered by an Italian chef with a "bellissimo" attached to it as he sampled his basil pesto.

"How is it possible that you have so much natural talent?" he quizzed. "You have a bright future. We might need to arrange some private lessons for you so I can share my secrets with you."

Pat smiled weakly. "Or you could share them with the entire class."

"I'd love some additional help—some private lessons," the woman seated on Pat's other side said. She looked up at him with an expression that Pat noticed, but had a hard time characterizing. Her tablemate's face held yearning, but something else, too. Disappointment? Wistfulness? She was one of the unadoring Pat had determined to talk to during lunch break—Garryn Monteith discouraged conversation at the worktables, telling his pupils they needed to concentrate and they needed to listen to his instructions—so even though they sat next to one another, Pat's only verbal interaction with her had been a quick exchange of names and the beginning of a conversation.

"I'm Suzanne Cummings," the woman had introduced herself.

"Pat Pirard. Are you one of our instructor's 'glass virgins'?" Pat had asked.

"No," Suzanne Cummings blushed. "Well, yes. This is my first peony class. But I was a star pupil many years ago in another one of Garryn's classes." Suzanne sighed loudly. "There's usually one, it seems."

"Was he right about you?"

"Ladies." Garryn Monteith had caught them talking and interrupted, ending their exchange. He smiled at them, but an added raised eyebrow had made it clear that what he was offering was mild chastisement. "Eyes and ears on me, please."

His response to Suzanne Cummings's appeal for extra help was clipped, cool, and flat. "Your work looks fine," he said. "I don't see a need for you to have private lessons."

"But I just thought…" Suzanne trailed off. Garryn had already moved up the row to the next woman in line, leaving Suzanne talking to herself.

Pat planned to talk to Suzanne during the lunch break,

but when it came, Suzanne disappeared into the bathroom before she could catch up with her. Pat waited by the door for as long as seemed reasonable, but Suzanne didn't reemerge.

As she moved toward the counter where others were helping themselves to lunch, Pat was waylaid by another woman.

"So what do you think of him?" the woman quizzed.

Pat shrugged. "It's too soon for me to tell much about him."

The woman puffed up her cheeks and expelled air in a huff. "His stories will never stop, especially when he gets into his 'genius' mode, but don't believe most of what he says."

"I'm Pat Pirard." Pat held out her hand. "Why is that?"

"Angela Grinardi." The woman's handshake was solid. "Because he's a thief and a cheat, albeit a charming one."

"I take it you've come to those conclusions after taking one of his classes?"

"No. I've just heard him bloviate in other settings. I thought I should take a class and see how he explains 'his secrets.' I can't wait until the last day of class when I get to prove his brilliant methods were stolen from someone with much more ability than he has in front of the entire group of Monteith admirers.

"It should be great fun to watch him squirm, especially since he's managed to get away with his thievery for so long and caused so much anguish in the lives of others. Not this time, though; I've got nothing to lose." Angela smiled as she savored her attack. "On day three, I'm going to destroy him."

"Pat, Angela," Joe called out to them cheerfully, "there's quinoa Greek salad, pasta primavera, or if you prefer, all the fixings to build yourselves spectacular ham sandwiches. Time's a-wasting. He's going to drag you back to class pretty soon, and it will be a long afternoon if you're hungry."

Pat was startled by what Angela said, but the woman was finished venting, turned her shoulder to Pat, and headed for Joe's array of food. She followed suit.

"Are these salads more of your creations, Joe?" Pat asked.

"Yep. I'm in charge of all the food around here. I even prepare Garryn's special meals. For this course he's going gluten free, hence the quinoa salad. Tomorrow we'll be having something corn-based for our star. What would you like?"

"The Greek salad looks good."

As he had in the morning, Garryn had assumed his place near the kitchen fireplace and was entertaining his gathered students, regaling them with even more stories, and feasting not only on salad, but on their charmed titters. Angela, full plate in hand, drifted toward the group.

Lillian's tinkling voice rose above the din. Pat couldn't make out what she said, but the timbre of what she heard caught Pat's attention, and she watched Lillian's dialog end with a hand placed familiarly on Garryn's arm. He covered her hand with his own and then removed it, smiling, not one of his practiced toothy grins, but softly and more intimately. Without the flamboyance that usually accompanied his smiles, his countenance seemed a bit sad, Pat thought.

Joe's ladle of quinoa Greek salad remained poised above Pat's plate as he watched his wife. "Oh, I'm sorry. Here I am telling you to eat and then not letting you." He was jovial once again as he delivered her salad, but once his task was finished, his eyes returned to his wife and his smile faded.

After one last glace at the bathroom door with its "occupied" sign still hanging from the doorknob confirming that Suzanne had not emerged, Pat took a seat next to Syda in the midst of the students.

Syda was glowing as she whispered to Pat, "This is such a great class. I've already learned so much. Aren't you having fun, too?"

"I am," Pat promised. "Syda, I can tell from the way we fit around the tables that I'm an extra. How did you manage to get me a place?"

"I've known Lillian forever; we artists tend to know one another. She let me add you to the class when I told her you were my best friend and that your life is kind of a calamity right now so you needed a new experience to take your mind off it. She's very sympathetic. She even gave me a deal on the class."

Pat closed her eyes and sighed. "Great. I love it that she thinks of me as a messed-up charity case."

"Well, your life is kind of messed up right now, so I

was only being truthful."

"I think I need to try the pasta primavera, too," Pat said as she spied Suzanne finally out of the bathroom and making a ham sandwich. She rose from her seat by Syda and headed back toward Joe.

"This is so good. May I try your other creation as well?"

"Of course. It's so nice to have one's efforts appreciated."

"Suzanne, isn't it?" Pat turned to her table-neighbor. "I'm enjoying this course immensely. You said you'd taken another class from Garryn. What other classes does he teach?"

"You can look him up online. Just Google him and you'll get his schedule." Suzanne turned her shoulder toward Pat. "Excuse me."

"You criticize the way she cut her glass?" Joe asked with a laugh.

"We sit next to one another. She seemed friendly initially." Pat shook her head. "Evidently she does think I did something to her."

Garryn Monteith clapped his hands. "Finish up, my darlings. We have spiders to play with this afternoon, and then we get to play with the kilns. It's going to be a big afternoon." His practiced smile was bigger than ever as he began leading his students back to the workroom.

Day two of classes began with Lillian Wentner opening

the huge kiln located in the L-shaped part of her studio. Each of the students had placed their cut glass on a tray able to withstand the 1440-degree temperature the kiln reached during the first phase of the melting and fusing of their glass layers. The kiln was large enough to easily accommodate the fifteen trays of work plus the improvised tray for Pat's work, a reminder that she was an extra in the class.

"Collect your trays, please," Lillian said.

Pat's improvised tray had gone in first and so she was the last to remove her work. It was exciting to see what had happened to the glass in the kiln overnight. The petals had fused and melted into natural-looking blends of color, and the stamens, which had started out as simple slices cut partway into a circle of bright yellow glass, were now separated and melted into spider-legged creatures with rounded feet.

"Oh, my darlings," Garryn Monteith effused, "you have all done wonderful work."

The morning session consisted of discussions about Ikea bowls and other stainless steel implements the students could use under their glass pieces to cause draping during the second firing. Garryn Monteith had several of his own pieces to show them and explained how he had achieved their looks. He promised that, with proper selections, their peonies would look as good as his when they were finished.

"Give it some thought, my darlings, and choose well, although I have to admit I've seen several students make what I considered to be 'daring' choices that produced outstanding results. Pick at least two stands for your petals so they drape well and have a natural look. Be thinking about how you want your flowers to look as you pick your drapers. When you are ready and back at your work stations, I'll show you how to place your glass to achieve the results you'd like. Visualize the look you want and be prepared; we are beginning the magic phase of what I will teach you. Aren't you excited, my darlings?"

After a short morning of picking and arranging, and Garryn Monteith's "tip of the day," that the tiniest dot of Super Glue was the artifice he used to hold pieces together until the kiln heat took over and melting began, each student was ready to carry their work to the kiln. Again, Pat went first in placing her creations at the very back of the kiln on the bottom row.

When all the pieces were inside the kiln, Lillian closed the door and secured it with a slide-lock. She set the firing timer and then said, "Lunch is ready. We'll be giving you some cheap wine with lunch because it's time for a mini celebration. The big one with champagne comes tomorrow, though, when your pieces are complete."

Pat had worked up a big appetite with all the decision-making and imagining that the class required, and she was eager to taste what Joe had come up with for their second-day meal.

"Joe, you've outdone yourself," Pat said as she let him place an aromatic bowl on her plate next to her butter-dripping cornbread. "Stew cooked in a pumpkin with cornbread on the side. Ten points for presentation and," she quickly picked up a spoon from an arrangement on the counter and sampled a spoonful of the savory stew that filled her bowl, "eleven for flavor."

"And the cornbread is a gluten-free recipe as the master demands," Joe added, a hint of resignation in his voice.

Pat noticed Suzanne Cummings was missing, probably in the bathroom again like the day before, and that the third member of the "not the biggest fans" set she observed yesterday morning was sitting by herself away from the devoted. She decided to take advantage of the situation.

"Hi. I'm Pat Pirard," she introduced herself. "I've met most of the students, but we are on opposite sides of the room…"

"Kandi Crusher. Don't say it. I had my name long before that stupid game came along."

"Is it your maiden name or your married name?"

"Both. When I went to high school, lockers were assigned alphabetically. George Crusher had the locker right above mine. We fell in love. We were high school sweethearts who got married—coming up on fourteen years now—so unless I divorce him, there's no hope for a name change. Believe me, I've thought about it, but the problem is I still love the guy."

"Do you have a middle name? Possibly you could use it."

"Mann. It was my mother's maiden name."

"That's even worse, isn't it?" Pat chuckled. "Have you considered using your initials? You'd be K.M. Crusher."

Kandi Crusher laughed heartily. "I have, but K.M. doesn't flow well, does it? Too reminiscent of a B.M."

"You're right," Pat laughed. "I guess you just have to flaunt your name. Never explain or apologize," Pat encouraged jauntily. "I couldn't help but notice that you're not by the fireplace hanging on Garryn Monteith's every word."

"No, I'm not. I notice you're not, either."

Pat chuckled. "True, but I was dragged here by a friend who gave me the class as a birthday gift, so I didn't arrive loaded with hero worship."

"Good friend. Much as I love my friends, I'd never give them an eight-hundred-dollar class as a birthday gift."

"That's how much this class cost?" Pat's mouth fell open. "I had no idea."

"Self-aggrandizing famous artists who think they have special skills can charge a lot for enlightening the rest of us lowly wannabes."

"You don't sound like a fan and yet you paid the price? Why did you do it?"

"Let's just say that I plan to get a lot out of the class, especially tomorrow."


"This afternoon you must be brave because we are going to drill holes in your spider designs, and I hope none of you will shatter what you have done." Garryn Monteith held up a hand in what to Pat had become his routine traffic-cop-stop pose. "No gasps, please. Never fear. I was just teasing. There's a trick to drilling glass, and with my guidance, I promise all your hard work will survive."

Pat's appreciation of Garryn Monteith's knowledge and ability to impart it to his students continued to grow during the morning in spite of, or perhaps because of, his over-the-top presentation. He was charismatic and a showman, and Pat was in the mood to let him entertain her. She had been enjoying the class more, too, because after she hadn't accepted his offer of private lessons, he had stopped insinuating himself into her personal space, and relegated her to being just one of "his darlings." She was ready to drill with fearless abandon.

But drilling holes proved to be taxing, and during the afternoon her teacher had again begun hovering and helping her too much, always with a hand on her shoulder and a whisper of encouragement in her ear. Her mind worked more on how she might move his over-reaching attentiveness along to the receptive Suzanne than on the task at hand.

By the end of the day, all necessary holes had been completed, and there had been no glass casualties among the students' spiders.

❋❋❋❋❋❋❋❋❋❋

"Today will be the most exciting day of our time together, because this is when I will share my secret techniques with you, my darlings," Garryn Monteith announced as the class gathered on the third day in the kitchen for coffee and Joe's creation of the morning:

cinnamon rolls.

Joe interrupted Garryn's speech to offer him a pastry. "Here you go, Garryn. I made this one especially for you. It's gluten free."

"Thank you, Joe, but I'll just have my usual coffee this morning. I'm watching my waistline." He postured before his students, twisting left and right with one hand on his stomach and the other behind his back as he posed and sucked in this gut.

"No you don't, Garryn. I put a lot of time and effort in this for you. I insist you at least taste it."

Joe's tone remained friendly, as did Garryn's, but Pat perceived a bit of alpha male jousting between them. Garryn was the one to back down.

"Well, since you went to all the trouble of making this just for me, and if you ladies don't think I look too fat"— murmurs of reassurance about his physique erupted from the audience—"perhaps just a bite or two." Garryn flashed his practiced smile as he took the pastry and made a show of taking a measured bite. "Yes, Joe. Very good. Possibly a little salty," Garryn said. He took a second bite and then placed the dish with his pastry on the fireplace mantel.

A few minutes later, Garryn clapped his hands. "It's time to go, my darlings. Aren't you excited to see your masterpieces? And aren't you even more excited for me to share my patented way of mounting them for display with you?" With that, the Pied Piper of glass lead his students toward the studio with Lillian bringing up the end of the procession.

As she had the day before, Lillian unlocked the kiln. She reached for the handle to open it, smiled at Garryn enticingly, and asked, "Should I?"

Garryn gently brushed her aside. "No, my dear, allow me. You know that being the first to look inside the kiln and seeing the beauty my darlings have created is my favorite part of being a teacher."

He placed both hands on the kiln door bar-handle and raised the door over his head. He released it and leaned forward to peer inside the kiln.

"App. App." He spun toward the group. "App. App." His mouth opened and closed rapidly. His eyes rolled up in their sockets, and he clutched his chest. His body convulsed, and then with a final gasp, Garryn Monteith collapsed facedown on the floor.

3

Pat's commiseration dinner was simple—spaghetti, broiled garlic bread, and green salad loaded with artichoke hearts and scallions to eat, and a decent Sangiovese to drink—and hastily put together. Joe took the heaping basket of warm bread from Pat who sat to his left at her kitchen table.

"I came running when I heard all the screaming," Joe said. "I knew that much commotion was more than a reaction to one of Garryn's witty stories or some disappointed student wailing because her peony was broken."

"I've never seen someone die before," Syda shuddered.

"His heart attack must have been massive, because when the EMTs got there, they told me he was already gone," Lillian added.

"So that's what it was?" Pat asked. "He had a heart attack?" She passed the spaghetti to Greg.

"That's what it looks like," Greg said. "The sheriff will check his medical history to see if he was under a doctor's care for heart issues. If he wasn't, and if he seemed healthy, an autopsy will have to be done."

"He wasn't that old," Lillian's shoulders hunched, "just a couple of years older than me. I've known him since we were both in our mid-twenties; he never complained to me about his heart or his health."

"Then he's probably headed to the autopsy table," Greg declared.

"The idea of him being taken apart on an autopsy table…" Lillian cringed and then focused her thoughts elsewhere. "I plan to hold what would have been the last day of instruction tomorrow. I know Garryn's techniques for attaching the flowers to stems. It's really not hard, and I've watched him explain how to do it so many times during the other classes he taught here. Most of the students said they can stay for at least a part of tomorrow; I'll teach an abbreviated session. We'll offer a full refund to Suzanne Cummings—she's local, but she's just too upset to come back—and to Patsy Jones who has to fly back to New Jersey on a red-eye tonight—and a big discount to everyone else. You two will come back, won't you?" Lillian asked Syda and Pat.

"I guess so," Syda said softly.

"Of course we will," Pat spoke with alacrity. "Come on, Syda, we have to see if we're good at this. How else will we know if we're destined to become the new Annieglass?"

※※※※※※※※※※

Joe had coffee and donuts waiting for the students in the studio the next morning. The coffee was as good as ever, but the donuts were store-bought and left in their pink bakery box, there for anyone who wanted one. Most students had coffee; few were up to eating a donut.

Lillian positioned herself where Garryn usually stood as he instructed the class, but unlike the way Garryn Monteith began his morning sessions with humor and lightness, she was somber.

"I just don't know what to say." Her voice caught and she dropped her head down. It took her almost a minute before she could continue. Others sniffed in sympathy with her and with the cognizance of what had happened the day before.

Joe put his arm around her shoulders and held her tight, offering physical as well as moral support.

"Garryn was a special friend and a talented artist. He would want us to finish his lessons. I won't be entertaining like he was, but I do know how to teach what he would have if he hadn't..." Lillian had to stop again, this time because of tears. Finally, she said, "If you'll go to the kiln and get your work..."

"Or if you want me to, if you'd rather not return to the alcove, I'll bring your peonies out to you," Joe offered. "You'll have to tell me what color flower I should look for and where your tray is in the kiln."

The students had placed their trays in the kiln by table in reverse order of where they sat. Table three and half of the second table were on the top shelf. The first few students took Joe up on his offer, and because of the placement pattern, it was easy enough for him to find each student's tray. But as more flowers came out of the kiln, students grew pluckier. Most of the rest were carried out by their creators.

The final flowers in the last row on the bottom shelf belonged to the two missing class members, Patsy Jones and Suzanne Cummings, and to Syda and Pat. Once Joe had removed the trays belonging to the other women, Syda and Pat were ready to get theirs.

Syda hung back as they approached the kiln. "I don't know if I can do it," she whispered to Pat.

"That's okay. I'll hand yours to you," Pat said.

She leaned far into the kiln, pulled Syda's tray toward her, and then picked it up, turned, and gave it to her friend.

Syda took it, grateful that she didn't have to touch the kiln.

Pat bent in again and began dragging her tray toward the front of the kiln. Her tray was a makeshift one and, after two firings, felt fragile compared to Syda's tray. She was concerned that it might crumple if she picked it up, so she slowly pulled her tray forward, letting it rest on the kiln bottom.

As her tray reached the forward edge of the kiln, Pat noticed a flutter of fine ashes. She hadn't seen ashes when she retrieved her tray after the first firing, and she feared that the ash was coming from her tray's bottom. Rather than risk the tray collapsing and causing a catastrophe, Pat took her two finished glass pieces out of the kiln and carried them back to her workspace.

She left the door up and her tray and forming bowls in the kiln. Lillian should know the makeshift tray had done its job, but barely, so she could design a better one or make any future student who had to rely on one aware of its shortcomings.

Lillian hadn't begun her instructions when Pat noticed Kandi Crusher was packing up her glass pieces. Kandi was at table three, about as far away from where Pat's workstation was as could be. Kandi looked up from packing her pieces in brown paper and gave Pat a finger-wiggle wave. Pat knew Kandi was signaling a goodbye, but her curiosity made her ignore that and interpret the wave as a gesture of invitation.

She left her place, walked quickly, and rounded the table as Kandi finished wrapping and began to place her glass pieces in a sturdy box.

"Are you leaving?" Pat asked. "I hoped we could talk again before everyone headed home."

"I'm out of here as soon as I finish securing my work."

"Do you have to catch a flight?"

"No. I live near San Francisco and drove down."

"Don't you want to see how to mount the flowers? You said you were looking forward to learning a lot today, didn't you?"

Kandi's mouth turned up on one side in a smirk, "I already know all there is to know about Garryn Monteith's 'secret system.' I planned to assemble my project before Garryn spoke, show everyone what I had done, and confront him in front of the class.

"I don't have to do that now, though, now that he's dead. And Lillian's just another one of the people he used while it was convenient for him. I have no need to make her look bad in front of the students, so there's nothing more for me to do here. Time for me to leave." Kandi hoisted her packed box. "It was nice meeting you, Pat."

"Me, too. I enjoyed meeting you, too."

Pat returned to her workspace as Lillian called the students to attention. "I have to talk fast because several of you have to leave before noon, so let's start immediately with how to use the stamen to hold everything together."

Pat spotted more and more students packing up as Lillian spoke. Angela left almost immediately, as did two others at her table. By the time Lillian finished her lecture and announced lunch was waiting in the kitchen, there were only six class members remaining to take her up on the lunch offer, only four not counting Syda and herself.

"I made tamales," Joe explained as the small band walked into the kitchen. "I made them yesterday when I thought we'd still have to be gluten free. Fortunately, tamales are forgiving about when they're cooked."

With only eight, the class and its hosts fit around the high L-shaped serving counter handily. The arrangement was conducive to chitchat. The conclusion of the course and the successful creation of wonderful glass peonies as different as their makers should have led to lively talk, but not much conversation happened. Everyone seemed relieved when it was deemed enough time had been spent over lunch and they could leave.

Pat watched Joe, and especially Lillian, hug each of the departing students and voice an "I'm so sorry" to them.

When only she and Syda remained, it seemed like the appropriate time to warn Lillian about the disintegrating tray.

"Lillian, I'm not complaining, especially since I know you let Syda sign me up after the class was full, but the tray you made for me, which worked fine for the first firing, is disintegrating now. There was ash coming off the bottom of it as I dragged it forward. I was afraid to pick it up for fear it would collapse and break my work." Pat smiled feebly, hoping she wouldn't leave her hosts and Syda thinking she was an unappreciative whiner. "Just a heads-up."

Lillian's forehead furrowed into a slight frown—not an angry one, but a curious one. "It's not the first time I've improvised trays. Ashes, you said? I don't see how that's possible. Will you show me what you mean?"

The four of them trooped out to the studio and into the kiln alcove. Everything was as Pat left it earlier.

"I pushed the tray back into the kiln, but see," she moistened her index finger and dabbed it in a bit of ash at the very front of the kiln. She held her finger aloft for the three others to see the spot of ash adhering to it. "There's not much, but enough that it made me worry about the integrity of my tray."

Lillian peered into the kiln and then picked up Pat's tray. She gave it a light one-handed shake and then turned it over and drummed on the bottom of it with the fingers of her other hand.

"It's fine; completely solid," she pronounced.

"Although, you are right, there is a bit of ash residue on the bottom of it. I have no idea where it came from, though, because it's not from the tray degrading. I wonder if one of the students accidently put something in the kiln, perhaps papers with sketches on them, something that adhered to the bottom of their tray without them noticing it? She shook her head, "I can't imagine any paper residue surviving the kiln heat, though. Oh, well, wherever the ashes came from, they need to go. Any ash residue could compromise future work."

Lillian placed Pat's tray in the storage rack near the kiln, found a hand brush, and swept the traces of ash out of the kiln onto the floor.

※※※※※※※※※※

Syda pounded on Pat's front door. "Pat, Pat, open up!" she shouted.

Dot rushed to the door and woofed a discreet, "Pat, are you hearing the knocking; I know your hearing isn't as good as mine?" instead of a bark announcing that there was a stranger at the door.

"Coming," Pat yelled over the pounding and woofing as she made her way from her guestroom-now-office, where she had been arranging furniture.

Between her eagerness to get inside and Dot dancing around her feet, Syda practically fell into the house when Pat opened the door.

"You are not going to believe this," Syda howled. "The

heart attack Garryn Monteith suffered wasn't a heart attack at all. He died from cyanide poisoning!"

"Cyanide poisoning?"

Syda's already-rapid delivery got even faster. "Uh-huh. You remember Greg said there would be an autopsy if Garryn didn't have a medical history? Well, he didn't, and there was, and the cause of death came back as cyanide poisoning."

Pat frowned. "But how did he get cyanide in him?"

Syda bobbed her head up and down, "Good question. Excellent question. He wasn't an outed spy with a suicide capsule, so someone must have given it to him. Greg says the sheriff is looking at murder.

"Everyone in the class is a suspect—us, too—but they've brought Joe in for a serious talk and are calling him a person of interest because he cooked our meals, and they think he could have slipped something into Garryn's food. The sheriff asked for the remains of the special cinnamon roll Joe made for Garryn the morning he died, but Joe said he disposed of it right after breakfast. Greg says that's what makes the sheriff think Joe is his prime suspect."

Pat shook her head. "You've seen films where someone is poisoned by cyanide, haven't you? It's fast. The victim goes down almost immediately. If Joe put cyanide in Garryn Monteith's food, he wouldn't have made it out of the kitchen. Besides, Joe is such a nice guy, and what motive would he have?"

"I don't know. All I can say is what Greg told me. It's

probably going to be on the news tonight." Syda licked her lips in anticipation. "I'm married to a deputy sheriff who tells me basics in investigations, but he always holds the juicy details back. I know the investigators always know things only the perpetrator knows. It's how they trip up the bad guys, and it's also how they know when a crazy confesses. I don't know why someone would confess to something they didn't do, but you'd be amazed how often that happens." Syda produced a big eye roll. "So maybe they have something on Joe that we don't know."

"You said everyone in the class is a suspect, not just Joe?"

"Yes. We'll all be getting a call or a knock on the door for a longer interview than the quick one we had the morning Garryn died, before anyone thought he was murdered. Of course, the deputy sheriffs will act like they just want to know if we noticed anything, but secretly I'm sure they'll be looking at us as murderers. Isn't that exciting?" Syda asked with gusto.

After a cup of coffee and some lemon pound cake Pat had made now that she had some free time, and a head poke into Pat's new office so Syda could suggest where her surfer painting should be hung, Syda left as hurriedly as she had arrived.

Pat used a nail and the heel of her shoe to pound it into her office wall and hung Syda's painting before she settled down in front of her computer. She was a researcher and old habits died hard; she smiled to herself as she looked up cyanide poisoning.

The circumstances of her research might be gruesome, but the process was familiar and, dare she think so, fascinating. Her research confirmed what she thought she knew. In a large enough dose to kill, ingested cyanide caused obvious distress within a minute or two and death within a few more minutes. There was no way Garryn could have led his band of students down to the studio, chatted at them, and made his way to the kiln without symptoms. He would have been complaining about dizziness or stomach pains, possibly even been disoriented.

Any way she considered it, if Joe had put cyanide in Garryn's food in a large enough dose to ensure a quick death, Garryn wouldn't have been fine until he clutched his chest and collapsed. Her research suggested that could only happen with inhaled cyanide.

Pat flipped from page to page of online data about cyanide poisoning before it occurred to her that she was using her laptop, not the computer at work. She chuckled out loud. *I hope no one ever reads my research history and starts thinking that I'm a killer.*

※※※※※※※※※※

Pat remembered meeting Officer Tim Lindsey briefly at a barbeque Syda and Greg had at their house last summer. At the time she thought he was cute, but since she was in a relationship and he was holding hands with an admiring blonde, her notice of him was casual and in passing. Now that he was sitting in her living room to interview her about Garryn Monteith's murder, she paid closer attention to him.

His eyes were very blue. His hair had reddish highlights, but had too much brown in it for him to be considered a redhead. He was tall, well over six feet, she guessed, and appeared muscled even through his sheriff's uniform jacket. His left hand didn't sport a wedding band. His question interrupted her observations.

"So, Miss, or do you prefer Ms. Pirard?"

"I prefer Pat."

His smile was quick and disarming. "Pat it is. You attended the entire class at the Wentners' studio?"

"I did."

"Did you notice anything unusual in Mr. Monteith's behavior during the course of the class?"

Pat giggled. "You'll have to be more specific. He was an unusual character. Charming, but a bit of a diva."

"I meant unusual behavior between him and any of the attendees or the Wentners."

Pat kicked off her shoes and tucked her feet under her as she sat on her sofa. "I don't know if I'd call any of the interactions unusual, but at the time I considered them noteworthy in some small way, which is why I remember them.

"The woman seated next to me, Suzanne Cummings, had a history with him and seemed as if she wanted attention from him. She seemed disappointed when it wasn't forthcoming. Then there was Angela Grinardi. She called him a thief and a cheat, although she didn't elaborate on what she meant. And Kandi Crusher…"

Officer Lindsey looked up from his notes, a bemused expression on his face.

"Yes, Kandi Crusher. We discussed her name at some length," Pat chuckled. "Well, Kandi admitted she wasn't a fan of his, but she paid eight hundred dollars to be in the class and then she left early saying she already knew about his 'secret system' for mounting the flowers we made, which was supposed to be a big part of the curriculum."

"Eight hundred dollars for a three-day class? I'm in the wrong profession," Officer Lindsey whistled through his teeth. "Did you notice anything unusual in his interaction with Joe Wentner?"

"There did seem to be some tension between them. Joe cooked for us. He's an excellent chef and he went out of his way to accommodate Garryn Monteith's gluten-free diet without making the rest of us unhappy with the food he prepared. Garryn Monteith didn't seem appreciative of Joe's efforts."

"Did Mr. Wentner serve the food?"

"Sometimes. He gave us choices, especially on the first day, but as the class progressed we were all offered the same meals."

"So you all ate the same food? And was it under your supervision the whole time?" Officer Lindsey smiled, "I sound like a TSA inspector, don't I?" He sing-songed, "Were you in possession of your bags at all times?"

"I understand what you're asking. We were free to pick our own servings, or if we were served, it was from a common container, and once served, there wasn't an opportunity to put anything in our food without us seeing it. I heard that Joe Wentner has become a person of interest. You want to know if he had the opportunity to slip something into Garryn Monteith's food, don't you?"

"That's what I'm asking. And you seem pretty observant to me, so do you remember him having an opportunity?"

Pat squirmed. "I like Joe and don't think he's a killer."

Officer Lindsey wasn't willing to let her off with just an opinion. "But you did notice something, didn't you?"

Pat nodded her head ever so slightly. "The last morning we were there, Joe prepared cinnamon rolls for the students. They weren't gluten free, of course, so Joe made a one-off creation for Garryn Monteith."

Officer Lindsey was a good interviewer. He knew when to be silent.

Pat pressed her lips together, knowing how what she was about to say would sound. "Garryn Monteith declined the pastry Joe made for him, but Joe insisted he at least try it. Garryn only took a couple of bites and complained the pastry was a bit salty.

"I've looked up ingested cyanide. Potassium cyanide could be put in food and might make it taste salty. But it doesn't make sense that Joe would be the one who poisoned him, because it would have been obvious where the cyanide came from. Joe would have to know he would be caught immediately. Besides, Joe would have had to bake a hefty amount of the compound into the pastry for it to kill, otherwise Garryn Monteith might have survived the poisoning, especially if he only ate a couple of bites of the pastry.

"With a big dose of ingested cyanide in him, Garryn Monteith would have been in extremis shortly after eating it, and he wasn't. He didn't exhibit any symptoms until he opened the kiln and leaned in…" Pat's words trailed off as she returned her shoeless feet to the floor and leaned toward Officer Lindsey.

"All indications were that he inhaled the cyanide. That would explain how quickly he died and why we all thought he had a heart attack." She pondered, "But Lillian was close to him and the rest of us were not far away, so why didn't any of the rest of us have problems if the kiln was somehow filled with cyanide gas?"

Dick Drinker called her the next day. "I'm not feeling guilty for downsizing you—I want to be perfectly clear about that—because you remember the decision was the Trustees', not mine. I want to remind you of that."

Pat held a quick debate with herself. Should she politely say nothing, or should she embrace the fact that she had nothing to lose? She went with the second choice. "You sure sound guilty," she stated pointedly.

"Not guilty; just bad. So I've been looking out for you. I found out about a job opening coming up in about a week. It hasn't even been announced anywhere yet."

"Really? What is this mystery position?"

"I have it on good authority that the County Library bookmobile driver is leaving. Do you know how to drive a stick shift?"

"I do, but I don't think I want a job where that's a make-or-break criterion."

"I'm just trying to be helpful, Pat. Think of it as something temporary to do until something better comes along. You've been unemployed for a week now, and I know you. You must be bored out of your mind with having nothing to do."

"Oh, I don't know. In just a week I've learned how to make glass peonies and become involved in a murder investigation."

"What? That guy who was killed at the glass studio— you were part of that?"

"Front and center. The authorities seem to think a very nice man who is part owner of the Glass House might be a murderer. It's ridiculous, but they aren't looking at the facts, at least not in the right way, so I'm thinking that I'm going to have to do some research to set them straight. That makes me much too busy to apply for a pity job. Thanks for thinking of me, though, Dick, and for trying to help."

As Pat hung up, it occurred to her that, even though what she told Dick was just an excuse for not being interested in the job he was suggesting, being at the Glass House when Garryn Monteith was killed had indeed made her part of a murder investigation. She found her involvement, however small, exhilarating. She wanted to dig deeper. *Just call me Private Investigator Pat,* she laughed out loud.

※※※※※※※※※※

Mark Bellows was the next attorney who called her.

"Pat, your name came up twice today, so I thought I'd see if you're available to do some research for me."

Pat hid her disappointment that Mark was calling about

business when she had hoped his was a personal call. "Who mentioned me?"

"Lillian and Joe Wentner have retained me because the authorities seem ready to charge Joe with first-degree murder. They gave me their class list, and I saw you were in the room when Garryn Monteith was murdered. Then I ran into Dick Drinker, who told me you're doing a little investigation about the murder on your own, so I figured maybe you could help me with Joe's case.

"I know it's short notice, but could we discuss what I have in mind over dinner tonight? Nothing fancy. I'll just pick something up at the Bruxo Food Truck—I hear he's doing Argentinian food for the next three weeks—so if that's okay with you, we can eat at my office. We can take our time and figure out how to work together on this." His tone softened from businesslike to something less formal. "And it will be a good excuse for me to see you, too."

It seemed to Pat that her first detecting job was to decide whether or not dinner with Mark was strictly professional or sort of a date. She came up with a rule: if there was wine involved, it was the latter. Mark had beer ready to accompany their meal, so she was still in a quandary as they ate and discussed Joe Wentner.

"The sheriff seems determined to make Joe a killer," Mark began, "and after interviewing him and his wife, I can see how they are going to present his motive. Lillian admits she's known Garryn Monteith for many years. She told me they dated briefly when they were both in their twenties, long before Joe came along, but right before the class started, Garryn sent her a couple of emails that she kept. They were pretty intimate and made it seem like Monteith expected them to be more than friends. The authorities think Joe saw the emails and are getting ready to say he considered Monteith a competitor for his wife's affections, felt threatened, and decided to get rid of him. What did you observe when you took the class?"

"There was some jockeying and poking going on between them, but it didn't seem like a big deal."

Pat paused, and Mark prompted her. "You noticed something, though, something you haven't told me yet, didn't you?"

"I noticed Lillian was pretty cozy with Garryn Monteith. According to Joe, Monteith taught a couple of classes a year at the Glass House. I don't know how he and Lillian conducted themselves during classes in the past, and her fawning may just have been part of the theatrics that went along with the course, but if Monteith's emails were suggestive and she seemed to be enjoying his attention, Joe might have felt threatened."

Mark sighed and took a long drink of his beer. "If it comes to it, I'm not going to look forward to having you as a witness telling a jury what you observed. Making it seem like Lillian welcomed Monteith's attention doesn't help Joe's cause."

"Then you need to delve into what else I noticed," Pat, ever hopeful that Mark might want them to connect outside of a working relationship, offered in a flirty tenor. "Joe wasn't the only one in the studio who had a problem with Garryn Monteith, and Lillian wasn't the only one who might have welcomed his attention.

"I sat next to a woman who told me she and Garryn had a thing in the past. Well, I may be overstating, but Garryn kind of came on to me, and Suzanne Cummings said he always picked someone in the class for 'extra help.' She said she had been that student once before, and, from the way she was acting, I believe she would have liked to be his star pupil—that's what she called herself—again."

"Speculation on your part, but interesting," Mark smiled a wicked little grin, "and believable, because I could certainly see Monteith hitting on you."

Pat hoped she wasn't blushing at Mark's comment. "There were also a couple of other students who had no fondness for Garryn Monteith. I mentioned their names to the deputy sheriff who interviewed me, and he wrote them down. Weren't you given that information?"

"Joe hasn't been charged yet, and those names wouldn't come out until discovery, so it's too soon for me to have been given them."

"Then I'll give them to you now: Angela Grinardi and Kandi Crusher. Mark, there's something that's bothering me about this murder that has nothing to do with motive," Pat said.

"What is it?"

"It's about means. According to my source—my friend Syda, whose husband is a deputy sheriff—what makes Joe so interesting to the department is that Joe gave Monteith something to eat shortly before his death. I heard the cause of death was cyanide poisoning, but I researched death by consuming cyanide, and Monteith didn't behave like someone who had ingested cyanide. He acted like someone who inhaled it. If you could prove Garryn Monteith died from inhaled cyanide, wouldn't that clear Joe?" Pat asked hopefully.

Mark shook his head thoughtfully. "Not really. If Monteith breathed in cyanide, that makes a stronger case for Joe being the murderer because he, and Lillian, of course, could have introduced cyanide into the kiln. A prosecutor will say Joe crept out to the kiln in the middle of the night and filled it with cyanide gas."

"Where would Joe have gotten the gas?"

"If the charge is murder one, they'll say he procured it before or right at the start of class. It's easy enough to buy tablets that could be modified to form gas. I've seen them for sale on Amazon, available for Prime delivery."

"Ick."

"So, I was going to say your job would be to introduce reasonable doubt by attributing motive to other people at the studio, but now it looks like you also better come up with a way someone other than Lillian or Joe could have filled the kiln with cyanide gas. I hope that doesn't seem like too much to ask of you for your first assignment as a private investigator, because I would like to hire you to do research for me. Shall we say at the same rate of pay you got from the Law Library?"

"Mark, that seems generous. We don't know if I'll be

any good at this."

"You are a highly capable woman. You'll be good at whatever you do. I'll expect updates by phone, but when you are ready to do a more in-depth report, may I take you to dinner—a real dinner out—to hear it?"

Pat smiled all the way home. When she got to her office, she ordered business cards printed with her newly invented job title, private investigator Pat, shortened to a catchy company name: "PIP Inc." She put her home address and phone number on them, and declared herself CEO of her one-woman company.

And then she went to work.

Pat never expected to solve the means issue first or so easily, but by the time she went to bed, she thought she had. She couldn't prove anything, but what she discovered warranted a call to Lillian and Joe in the morning and then possibly to Mark.

She struggled to believe it was as easy to procure cyanide as Mark said it was, so she had begun her research by looking up "sources of cyanide." Because of the way the internet worked, the Grenfell Tower fire in London in 2017 that killed over eighty residents came up. She was intrigued and opened the page; just a little macabre side diversion before she went back to serious investigating. What she read sent her off her planned research path.

Newspaper accounts said several survivors of the fire had been treated for cyanide poisoning, and autopsies of victims who were not burned in the fire revealed they died because of inhaling cyanide. The tower's cladding was blamed. The article cited other common sources of cyanide: fruit pits and apple seeds, plastics, carpeting, and, Pat read, Super Glue.

*Super Glue.* Garryn Monteith taught his students how to use the tiniest dab of Super Glue to hold glass pieces together before firing melted them into position. Every student had received a list of required materials for the class, which included the glue. No one would have been aware of it if a student carried several more tubes of Super Glue than the one tube necessary for class. They were small and could have fit unnoticed in a purse or materials bag filled with the requisite glass cutters, snippers, and wires.

Pat hurried to her garage and dragged her materials bag out of a cupboard where she had tossed it after the class. She felt around inside the bag, drawing blood when she poked her finger on the end of her roll of sharp-cut wire. Her leftover glue came in a metal toothpaste-like tube, but was much smaller. It had a pointed plastic cap, almost as large as the tube, which was already impossible to pull off after only a few days. She put her bleeding finger in her mouth and carried the tube back to her desk for a closer look.

Pat held the tube with its tiny print under her desk light and inhaled sharply when she read the first three words on it. "WARNING: Contains Cyanoacrylate." *Cyanide.* Further lettering warned against inhaling vapors and said to call a physician if symptoms occurred after inhalation.

She didn't sleep even after she turned off her computer for the night. She formulated a list of questions to ask Lillian and Joe the next morning as soon as the clock told her it was late enough to call them without shocking them awake.

Pat held off until 8:00 a.m. and then dialed their number. The phone rang and went to the answering machine. She tried again at 8:30 and then at 9:00 with the same result. Where they in the studio working or conducting a class? Pat knew Lillian did teach classes herself, and Joe might have been helping her—and, Pat reasoned, they might not have a phone turned on out there. She made the decision to go see them in person.

"You're in charge," she explained to her Dalmatian as she picked up her purse. "I won't be gone long."

Dot whimpered pleadingly.

"No, you can't come with me. There are squirrels in the woods and I wouldn't want to risk you chasing one and getting lost."

Dot flopped on the floor with her head draped on crossed paws and whined again.

"I know I'm asking a lot of you and it is Wimsey's turn to be in charge, but unlike his namesake, Lord Peter, he's so unreliable. Besides, he's a cat and you know how cats can be." Pat rubbed Dot's head. "I promise there'll be a walk at the beach later today as a reward for your understanding."

Dot didn't raise her head, but at least she stopped being vocal in her complaints about the unfairness of having to stay at home.

Pat pulled her sunburst-yellow car into the Wentners' driveway and drove down it toward the studio, proud that her vehicle was more colorful than any of the flowers, real or glass, that adorned the garden in front of their farmhouse. She parked, walked to the studio door, and tugged. It was locked fast. She turned to the farmhouse, walked up the front steps, and knocked. There was no response. Finally, Pat walked along the front porch until she came to the kitchen door, the one used by Garryn Monteith and the students the week before, and knocked again.

A disheveled Lillian, barefoot and still dressed in the white flannel nightgown embroidered with tiny pink rosebuds she had worn to bed the night before slowly pulled the door open a crack. When she recognized Pat, she pulled the door open wide, collapsed into her arms, and began to sob.

"They arrested Joe early this morning. He was handcuffed and put into a patrol car, and they read him his rights. Oh, Pat, what are we going to do? Joe didn't kill Garryn. Why won't they believe him?"

"Have you called Mark Bellows?"

"That's the first thing I did. He's trying to arrange bail. The charge is first-degree murder," Lillian's gulping sobs began again, "he said he may not be able... he may not be able to get Joe out of jail."

"May I come in? I have some questions for you. Your answers might help prove Joe's innocence."

"Of course!" The hand Lillian waved as an invitation shook as she motioned for Pat to come inside.

"I'd offer you coffee, but I've already had so much this morning. Would you like green tea?" Lillian asked.

"I'd love some. Lillian, how hot did the kiln get the night before Garryn's death?"

"We fired for the second time slightly lower than the first time, at about 1300 degrees. Why?"

"Hot enough," Pat said triumphantly. "Do you remember the ashes in the kiln?"

"Umm," Lillian looked puzzled and frowned slightly. Then her expression changed. "Yes. Yes, I do. There weren't many; you thought your tray was flaking."

"That's right. Now, I think they came from Super Glue tubes."

Lillian seemed perplexed as Pat went on. "Aluminum mostly melts, but if the temperature is hot enough it will oxidize and leave ashes. Thirteen-hundred degrees is more than enough for that to happen."

"I don't understand."

Pat ignored Lillian's confusion and continued with her questions.

"Could anyone besides you and Joe have opened the kiln and put Super Glue tubes in it?"

"Yes, I guess," Lillian said with some hesitation. "A kiln is just a super oven; it takes a while for the temperature to ramp up. At the start of the warm-up it's not very hot and, if you're quick and close the kiln again right away, it doesn't affect the temperature more than a few degrees. I've done it myself, opened the kiln after I started firing, to slide in a forgotten piece. Opening it didn't affect any of the work being fired."

"Do you lock the studio at night?"

"We do." Lillian had an "aha" moment. "Now I see what you're asking, but someone slipping in at night couldn't have opened the kiln. It would have been too hot by then. It would have to have been opened soon after firing began."

"Like when we were having lunch?" Pat asked.

Lillian nodded her head. "That would be the perfect time to do it."

"So here's what I'm thinking," Pat explained. "All of the students had Super Glue for the class, and most could have slipped back to the studio during the lunch break. They could have covered their return by saying they forgot something in the studio or slipped out during a bathroom break. All attention was on Garryn Monteith anyway, so most of us wouldn't have noticed a fellow student's short absence.

"I didn't hover or hang on Garryn's every word. I spent some time talking to Joe. Between him serving the students and our conversation, I might be able to account for his movements—alibi him, as it were—and introduce a whole class full of other potential murderers."

Lillian began to cry softly. "Pat, how can I thank you?"

"Drink your tea. I have a few more questions," Pat instructed. "Is it the usual procedure for the class instructor to open the kiln? I'm asking because you opened it the first day, and you seemed about to open it the second day until Garryn stepped in and insisted on being the first to look inside it."

"Usually I would open the kiln every day I taught a class or had another instructor in, I guess because it's in my studio, but you're right, Pat. Whenever Garryn taught, he opened the kiln after the last firing. We had an arrangement. I was to ask him if I should open the kiln and he would say no, that he wanted to do it. It was part of his presentation and his theatricality."

"That's been his pattern before?"

"Always."

"Did Joe ever come into the studio when Garryn taught?'

"He wouldn't stay for long, but he often drifted in and out for a few minutes at a time during Garryn's classes."

Pat wasn't sure she liked what Lillian just told her, however she kept her misgivings to herself. They could prove exonerating or damning for Joe's case, and she wanted to hear Mark Bellows's opinion before saying more.

"Lillian, you keep class records, don't you, names, addresses, email addresses, phone numbers, credit card information?"

"Not all of those things. I do keep names and email addresses and sometimes mailing addresses if students don't share their email, so I can let them know about upcoming classes."

"I'll need a copy of all the information you have from the class."

"What are you going to do with it? I always promise we don't share information with anyone."

"I'm not going to share it. I'm going to find out who had a motive for killing Garryn Monteith. That's the best way to exonerate Joe."

Lillian produced a class list from her laptop and printed out a copy for Pat. "I don't understand how you'll be able to solve a murder from this," Lillian said as she handed the sheet to Pat.

"Neither do I—not yet—but I plan to figure it out."

Pat used her cell phone to call Mark's office as she drove along Highway 1 toward Santa Cruz. When she asked to speak to him, his receptionist informed her he wasn't expected back in the office for most of the day.

"Could you get a message to him?" Pat asked. "I have some interesting information for him about the Joe Wentner case, too much to leave as a message. Would you ask him to call me?"

Mark called just as Pat reached home. She sat in her car while they talked.

"My receptionist says you need to speak with me. I'm swamped right now; did you hear Joe Wentner was arrested? He's being arraigned this afternoon so I have a lot to do."

"I have some information that may affect the case against him."

"Then let's meet for dinner tonight. Oswald's at 7:00? I'll make a reservation."

Even though she knew the planned dinner was definitely a working consultation, Oswald's served wine. Pat decided it was time to wear her green dress.

When she went inside, Pat tried to begin researching her suspects list, which was essentially the glass class list with three candidates in prime position, but lack of sleep after last night's late finish, the excitement of contemplating another dinner with Mark Bellows, and thinking her business card—set up hastily and more in fun than in earnest—might portend her future, fuzzed her brain and her process.

She struggled to focus, and Dot's displeasure with her didn't help. Dot complained about being neglected as only a dog could and demanded her promised trip to the beach. By the time they got home, early afternoon had passed and Pat gave in to her tiredness.

There were certain advantages to being unemployed and a taking a midday nap was one of them, so she told herself that she wanted to hear what Mark thought of her first bit of research before spending time in front of a computer screen. She curled up on her sofa under her favorite quilt and wiggled until she was extremely comfortable. Wimsey climbed on her hip, but even his pumping and purring couldn't keep her awake.

The walk at the beach had so exhausted Dot that she didn't move from her dog bed as Pat, newly refreshed from her power nap and shower and sporting perfect hair, freshly reapplied makeup, and wearing the green dress that looked even more impressive than she remembered, left the house at 6:30 without doing any more investigation.

"I hope you have some good news for me," a haggard-looking Mark said as he and Pat were shown to their table at Oswald's. After seating them, the server shook out her napkin and placed it on her lap. Pat smirked. Good service was appreciated; being made to feel like a child was not. Pat felt only slightly better when the server did the same thing to Mark.

"I know him. I used to think he did his napkin thing because I looked forgetful, but that's just what he does," Mark laughed. "Don't take it personally. He said he trained in an upscale New York restaurant, and he's trying to raise the standards in Santa Cruz. I suggested he try for a job at Shadowbrook with its chilled forks, but he says he likes it here.

"I'm surprised to hear from you so soon," Mark said after the server presented them with menus.

"I didn't expect to have anything for you this soon, either. And I may not, so don't get your hopes up too high. It's just that I found something that may throw a room full of suspects into the mix. I think I know how Garryn Monteith was murdered, and it had nothing to do with him ingesting cyanide."

"You said that yesterday. You didn't think he could have eaten poison without showing immediate distress."

"I did. The problem was, if he didn't ingest cyanide, how did it get somewhere where he could inhale it? I believe the answer is Super Glue, and if I'm right, everyone in the class becomes a viable suspect because we all had both the glue and access to the kiln, where it was placed."

Mark closed his eyes and held up his hands. "Whoa. You're losing me."

"We all used Super Glue on our flowers, and Super Glue contains cyanide. We put a dab of it on our pieces to hold them in place before firing. It burned off in the kiln, leaving nothing behind but a harmless amount of vapor, which dissipated the moment the kiln was opened."

"Then how could such tiny amounts of vapor kill Monteith?"

"It couldn't. It would have taken the cyanide in several full tubes to be deadly. I think someone put multiple tubes in the kiln right at the front of it so Garryn Monteith inhaled a lethal dose when he opened the kiln and leaned in for a look at our flowers."

"Maybe I'm just tired, it's been a looong day,"—Mark drew out the length of the word—"but I don't understand. Wouldn't there be melted Super Glue tubes left in the kiln? And how could someone put glue in the kiln without being observed?"

"Lillian gave me the answers to both of those questions. The kiln was turned on for firing just before we left the studio at lunchtime. Anyone could have slipped out to the studio and opened the kiln while we were on our lunch break. There's nothing tricky about locking and unlocking the kiln, and the temperature fires up gradually, so it could have been opened soon after the firing process started.

"As for the tubes, they would have been oxidized by the heat inside the kiln. I was a last-minute add to the class and there weren't enough trays for me, so Lillian improvised mine. After Garryn Monteith died, when I slid my tray forward to take it out of the kiln, I observed some ashen residue and thought it was coming from my tray. I told Lillian, but she assured me that wasn't possible. We looked inside the kiln and discovered there was a bit of ash right at the kiln door. I think it was from oxidized tubes of Super Glue.

"Lillian said she usually opens the kiln for classes, but Garryn Monteith opened it after the second firing, right before his alleged heart attack. Lillian started to open the kiln, but he brushed her aside, opened it, and stuck his head inside for a first look at our projects. That's when he collapsed."

"So you think that's when he inhaled cyanide?"

"I do. I can't prove it, though."

"We wouldn't have to prove it. We just have to convince a jury that's what happened."

Mark smiled for a moment, but his smile faded quickly. "You may be exactly right about how Monteith was poisoned, but if you are, a good prosecutor might still make Joe look like the killer. 'Couldn't Joe have been the one to slip out and put the tubes in the kiln?' he'd ask."

"I talked to Joe during the lunch break. He was busy serving lunch. He didn't leave the house," Pat said.

"'You talked to him for the entire lunch break? You never let him out of your sight?' That's what the prosecutor's next question would be."

"Well, no. Not exactly. I spoke with one of the other students, with Kandi Crusher, later in the break, but I think I glanced at Joe often enough to know he was always in the kitchen."

"Gotcha. Or rather, got Joe. 'Ms. Pirard, is it possible that you became so involved in your lunch conversation with Ms. Crusher that you missed Joe Wentner being absent from the kitchen for just a few minutes? Since he is so familiar with the studio, couldn't he have moved quickly and been back before you missed him?' That's what you'd be asked, and your answer would reluctantly be, 'It's possible,' wouldn't it?"

Mark perked up. "I just had a great idea, a counter to the possibility Joe put the glue in the kiln. He loves his wife, right? I could argue Joe would never risk putting the tubes in the kiln. Suppose Lillian had opened it; he wouldn't have taken the chance."

Pat squirmed. "I wanted to talk to you about that. Lillian said she usually did open the kiln after the first firing, but she told me Garryn Monteith always opened the kiln after the final firing. She said that was part of his showmanship. I asked her if Joe was ever in the studio during Garryn's classes and she said he sometimes was. If he had seen Garryn make a big deal about opening the kiln on the last day…"

A defeated Mark said, "Lillian may convict him."

"Then I better get to work finding the real killer in the class."

6

"So how did it go?" Syda crooned.

"I told you we were having a business dinner."

"You told me you liked him."

"I do."

"You weren't just saying that so I'd back off trying to find Mr. Right for you, were you?"

"What would be the point of that? I know you'll keep trying until the day you are my matron of honor."

"You said you were going to wear your green dress. That doesn't sound like strictly business to me."

"Well, it was."

"Did you invite him in?"

"We had separate cars so there was no would-you-like-to-come-in-for-coffee chatter."

"Did he walk you to your car?"

"Yes, he did."

"And was there a little goodnight kiss at the car door?"

"No, there wasn't."

Syda heaved a disappointed sigh. "Then when are you going to have dinner with Greg and me so we can introduce you to Greg's fellow deputy sheriff?"

"Not anytime soon. Remember, I have been officially

hired by Mark Bellows to work on Joe's case. I have to look good for the sake of future business, not to mention Joe. I'm going to be busy for the foreseeable future."

"You have to eat even when you're working."

"No, Syda. No dinner. Not now." Pat tried to sound as firm as she could without hurting Syda's feelings.

"*She's disappointed, but she'll live,*" Pat told herself after their conversation ended. She had too much on her mind to entertain guilty feelings for not making her best friend happy.

Pat still had Dick Drinker's number in her phone. She was going to need his permission for what she wanted to do, and she wanted to ask a favor while he was still feeling guilty for downsizing her. No guilt for Syda, useful guilt from Dick. She smiled; interesting how guilt worked.

"Dick, it's Pat Pirard," she greeted him when he answered his private line. "I need to ask you for a tiny favor."

"What do you need?"

"Your permission to access a database that's at the Law Library, but not available to non-employees."

She could feel his frown over the phone. "Why and which database?"

"You shared my employment situation with Mark Bellows—thank you for that—and he has kindly hired me to help him work on a defense for a client. I'll be doing some background checks on suspects. I need access to the LexisNexis database with its people finder and background checker."

"That's not something that has privileged information in it, is it?"

"No, I wouldn't ask for anything confidential or privileged," she giggled charmingly. She didn't add that she might if she needed that kind of information now that she had ordered business cards proclaiming her a private investigator, but what she wanted was only access to the US Persons Location and Public Records section of a data bank. "Everything in the database is a public record. It's just awfully handy because it's all in one place. It'll only take a few minutes to get what I need."

"Okay. I'll call Jefferson and tell him I told you it's okay with me if you use the database, unless he has a problem with it. If he agrees to it, you'll be good to go."

"Thank you, Dick. I'll go to the Law Library this afternoon."

"High-five," Pat said to Dot, who had been sitting near her feet while she was on the phone. She had trained her Dalmatian to elevate a paw on hearing that phrase, and she tapped her pet's paw with gaiety as Dot responded.

Pat had already scanned the information Lillian sent her and narrowed the field of interesting subjects to three: Kandi Crusher, Angela Grinardi, and Suzanne Cummings. All had made comments to her that were in one way or another thought-provoking. Certainly other class members might have had suggestive things to say about Garryn Monteith, too, but she had to start somewhere. So for her first detecting gig, she decided to limit her work researching class members to the three of them. Armed with her suspects list, she was ready to go back to her old haunt.

Force of habit almost made Pat aim her car toward her old parking spot. She turned left rather than right just in time to avoid having to do a backup maneuver out of the employee lot and into the melee of general public parking at the County Building. It would have hurt to see who had assumed her plum labeled space—she was sure it hadn't been turned over to Jefferson—so she convinced herself it was a good thing she had to park with all the people doing ordinary business at the five-story building.

By the time she had made her way to the Law Library door, high heels again clacking down the long concrete hall on the way there in what was a homely sound to her ears, Pat was ready to greet Jefferson, her newly elevated assistant, in what was now his domain, not hers. At least she thought she was.

Her face must have betrayed her, even though she plastered on a brave smile, because he jumped up from behind the reception desk and crushed her in a consoling hug.

"It's *so* good to see you," he overstated.

"I've only been gone a few days."

"But it seems like forever. Mr. Drinker called and said you'd be stopping by to use the LexisNexis if it was alright with me—like it wouldn't be—and I told him of course it would be. Would you like to use my office to set up?"

"Thank you. That would be perfect."

Stepping across the threshold of what had been her office and not being greeted by Syda's surfer painting and her rainbow files was harder than she thought it would be. Jefferson had already redecorated the office and made it his with old movie posters, the most prominent a *Pulp Fiction* poster signed by Quentin Tarantino. Her eyes lingered on it because she was afraid to look left or right to see what had become of her judges.

"Isn't that one great?" Jefferson effused. "My husband got it for me for my birthday. I absolutely love it."

"Yes. It's very special."

Jefferson was nothing if not a kind man. "Well, for now let's call this 'your office,' yours to use as you see fit for as long as you need. Oh, and I like the arrangement you made of our retired judges. I'm keeping them just the way they are." He closed the office door and returned to the seat behind the intake counter.

Pat logged on to the LexisNexis program, relieved to see that the program password hadn't been changed. It was a detailed search engine that compiled several public records for law enforcement and government agency groups to save them hours of search time. Almost thirty categories were examined—everything from boat license registrations to real property records—with a myriad of more specialized and not necessarily easy-to-find public records. And there were other categories on the database, as well. Information about potential relatives, business associates, neighbors, employment records, legal entanglements, cell phone numbers, and an address summary were also part of the reports. Researching such records was akin to the sort of work an FBI agent might do for a background check, and it was irresistibly at Pat's fingertips.

She wasn't yet certain what information might prove useful to her, so she intended to print out everything the program could tell her about her three classmates. As she typed, she added two other names she knew she needed to research: Joe Wentner, because tracking his background might help Mark Bellows prepare a defense, and Garryn Monteith because understanding the murder victim was important.

Almost as an afterthought, Pat added Lillian Wentner's name to her search. Pat wasn't sure why she made the last-minute addition of Lillian's name, but a little voice in her head told her that she had heard something curious about Lillian that she couldn't remember at the moment, and that it was a good idea to add her name.

Pages printed in another location in the library and when Pat saw the amount of documentation her six names generated, she was glad she had brought her leopard-print briefcase with her. She scooped the documents into her briefcase and hoped she could slip out with just a wave while Jefferson was occupied helping a patron. She had almost made it to the Law Library door when Jefferson called her name.

"Pat, that was fast. Are you finished already?" he asked.

"I got what I needed." She patted her briefcase. "Now I have to go home and make sense of it."

"Mr. Drinker tells me you're working on something for Mark Bellows...?" Jefferson, kind, but a gossip, dangled the end of his sentence.

"That's right. I'm a private investigator now."

"How cool is that! You astound me. What an amazing juggler you are, working here and putting in all the hours you need to become a PI?"

"Hours?"

"Yes. It takes three thousand hours of supervised experience to become a licensed PI. I looked into it once. I was trying to impress a date and thought it would sound good if I said I was a PI. A librarian wasn't the image I was going for then," he chuckled and made little keystroke finger movements. "I wanted to be a he-man, and being a PI sounded so thrilling, so macho.

"Oh, why am I saying this to you? Of course you know how it works. You can't become a PI just by saying you are, can you?" he chortled. "Now I have to know, are you a master juggler or did you have your license before you started here?"

Pat smiled and evaded answering directly. "Let's just say I have many hidden talents."

Jefferson's face, which a moment before glowed with unabashed admiration, shifted through confusion into concern. "You are licensed, aren't you?" he stuttered. "I mean; you couldn't use the LexisNexis program if you weren't an employee here or licensed, even if Mr. Drinker..." His voice quivered ever so slightly. "I don't think you would meet the program's criteria for use if you weren't licensed. It wouldn't be legal, and Mr. Drinker said it was my decision..."

Pat twittered. "Don't worry. I have business cards and everything."

Jefferson looked reassured.

Pat feared his relief was only going to be momentary. "I've got to hurry, bye-bye," Pat said quickly as she pushed open a massive Law Library door.

Her heels clicked double time as she rushed down the hall and out to her car. She drove out of the lot hurriedly, half expecting to hear a siren wailing for her to stop and surrender her ill-gotten documents before she was taken to jail, and hoping she had selected the right candidates for her investigation, because she knew she wasn't going to get a second chance to research them with LexisNexis.

✳✳✳✳✳✳✳✳✳✳

Syda had already finished one glass of wine that Pat knew about and was sipping her second. "I'm so glad you asked me to solve Garryn Monteith's murder," she intoned solemnly.

Even a modest amount of alcohol amplified Syda's dramatic tendencies, and the fact that she had skipped lunch wasn't helping. Pat hoped the chuck roast would be ready soon.

"And I'm so glad you came over for dinner with me. I wasn't looking forward to eating alone. It's just too bad that Greg and his partner had to pull a double shift, or I could have invited him, too, and you could have met him."

"I...we...have work to do. Tonight wouldn't have been a good night."

"What do you want me to do, exactly?"

"Take a report and highlight anything you think deserves a closer look in yellow," Pat instructed. "For example: I don't think the number of boats or aircraft one of our suspects owns matters, but NODs..."

"What's a nod?"

"...notice of default might, and real property might. Bankruptcy might, too, and certainly potential relatives, business associates, personal associations, neighbors, and employment records need to be highlighted."

"What about criminal filings? Trouble with the law sounds juicy."

"That, too."

"Oh, this is going to be fun. Could I have Garryn's file? I'd love to see what dirt the program turned up about him."

Pat handed Garryn Monteith's file to Syda without hesitation. Syda could play detective, but Pat would go over the pertinent parts of all the reports in the morning.

A few minutes later Syda announced, "Garryn Monteith was a very bad boy. He has all sorts of legal actions filed against him. The IRS wanted money, and the State of California and the Feds were after him, and a couple of business partners sued him, and then it looks like he filed bankruptcy." Syda poked through more pages, her yellow marker flying.

"Never mind. It looks like a new Garryn rose from the

ashes like a phoenix. He seems to have gotten his act together after a while and made a lot of money and bought property. I guess his legal problems history was just because he was an artistic youth who didn't know how to handle money."

Syda pulled the hair stick out of her informal bun, retwisted her hair, and then repined it higher up on her head. "I can relate to that. If I wasn't married to Greg, I'd be a starving artist, too. It's nice to know that people other than Grandma Moses and Georgia O'Keefe can come into their full artistic expression once they are more mature. There's hope that I'll be a raging success yet."

"And I can say I knew you when," Pat teased.

Syda held out her hand. "Since I'm finished with Garryn Monteith, let me see Suzanne Cummings's file. I hope there's nothing bad about her past in it. I liked her."

"She talked to you? She wouldn't have anything to do with me."

"That's because you were a threat; Garryn was too interested in you. I'm happily married so I wasn't."

"When did you talk to her? I never saw her around at lunch time."

"No, she wasn't. She spent lunch breaks in the bathroom crying and then trying to redo her makeup so she didn't look like she had. It was sad, really, how she would arrive in the morning all happy and chatty and convinced Garryn would suddenly look at her—see her—and be interested in her again. She told me she still loved him, even though it had been many classes since he loved her back.

"It never happened for her, though. She'd spend the morning watching him flirt with you and be ready for a good cry by lunch break. She never gave up, though. I guess you'd say she never learned. But true love is like that, isn't it?"

The oven timer buzzed. Syda smacked her lips. "Thank goodness. I'm famished already and now all this detecting has made me extra hungry."

Pat was glad the interruption meant she didn't have to answer Syda's question. She knew love could die. And she didn't care to enlighten her romantic friend that after hurt, love often became anger before it did.

Her cursory review of the LexisNexis files of her classmates last night with Syda hadn't produced any startling results. Based on the reports, the lives of the three women seemed pretty mundane. There were no criminal proceedings to note; names changed because of marriages; relatives seemed to be husbands, children, parents, brothers, and sisters: all the connections ordinary people had. None appeared to be hiding a guilty secret or a suspected axe murderer history.

With the start of a new day, Pat settled at her desk with the six files stacked neatly to her left and her mug of coffee still steaming even after she added a hefty pour of half-and-half to it on her right.

Wimsey had settled on an office window ledge, his routine on sunny days, to soak up warm rays. He'd fall off the ledge with a start once the sun lulled him to sleep, but he'd land on the broad back of a padded chair set under the window and fall asleep again almost instantly. She'd seen his fall repeat many times, and after she had chuckled at his awkward dismount, she realized he always positioned himself so he would end up on the chair back. Her opinion of him had changed from one of mocking to one of great respect. He now seemed to her to be a clever and possibly brilliant cat.

Dot joined them in her office just after Wimsey plunged, as if her sensitive ears could hear the subtle sound of a cat landing on padding, and had taken up a position at the base of the chair. Pat was comfy and ready to work.

She began with Garryn Monteith's file. Syda was right; early on he hadn't handled his finances well. He had skipped paying state taxes in California, where his address history said he lived until he was thirty, and he hadn't filed with the IRS for a period of time. When those two oversights became apparent, both the State of California and the IRS had filed claims and received judgments against him.

Two other actions had been taken against him, but those had been dismissed. Looking at Syda's highlighted marks, Pat noted both men who had filed failed lawsuits came up as business associates of Garryn Monteith's. They were Peter Mann Frieberg and Leonardo Grinardi. Pat stopped reading abruptly as she hit Leonardo Grinardi's name.

She grabbed Angela Grinardi's file from the stack and flipped it open to the potential relatives section. The first name that came up under first-degree relatives was Leonardo Grinardi. His file had a red triangle with an exclamation point after his name. Pat knew what the symbol meant. It indicated the person referenced was deceased.

Pat scanned the rest of the information about Leonardo Grinardi and compared it with Angela Grinardi's file. Leonardo was born four years before Angela. They shared a residence in Maryland at the time of his death at age fifty-one, and there were three names listed with the same residence address: two girls and a boy who would have been twenty-two, twenty, and seventeen at the time of their father's—and yes, she had every reason to assume they were his and Angela's offspring—death a year ago.

Pat thought back to her conversation with Angela in the Wentners' kitchen. If she remembered correctly, Angela knew Garryn Monteith, although she said she hadn't taken his class before. She called him a thief and a cheat and said she looked forward to watching him squirm.

A shiver went up Pat's back. She may not have remembered some of what Angela said precisely, but she absolutely remembered one thing Angela stated. She pledged to destroy Garryn Monteith on the third day of class. Pat was sure she remembered Angela's promise correctly because its delivery was venomous. It had impressed her.

And now she had found a connection between Angela and Garryn Monteith. Angela's late husband had sued him and lost. Was that enough connectivity to provide a motive? Was it enough to make Angela a suspect in murder? Probably not, but it was enough to excite Pat's curiosity.

The first thing she wanted to know was why Leonardo Grinardi had sued Garryn Monteith. With her background as a law librarian, she knew just where to find that information. Pat logged on to the Public Records Access to Court Electronic Records site. Even though the suit had taken place years before, details about it would be there. And unlike LexisNexis, at ten cents per page the database was cheap to use and only required registration and billing information to access. Pat smiled. *No restricted access, no user reviews and secret handshakes.* Perfect.

Dot gave out a soft woof and left the room. She returned a minute later with her red leash in her mouth. She sat dutifully for a few seconds before she nudged Pat's leg.

"Okay. Cross your legs and give me just a few more minutes and then I'll take you out for a bathroom walk."

Dot gave Pat a classic sad-eyed-disappointed-dog look and dropped the leash at Pat's feet, seemingly resigned to obeying her mistress.

Pat was into the database and reading in a few minutes. The suit complaint stated that Garryn Monteith had stolen Leonardo Grinardi's patented system for attaching glass flowers to support systems in a way that enabled the glass portions to be significantly larger and heavier than previously possible.

The Judge hearing the case accepted Garryn Monteith's statement that, even though they were business partners, both men had small studios and worked independently. He stated that he had created his own highly similar system independently and without observation of Leonardo Grinardi's work. The judge agreed and ruled against the charge of patent infringement. Pat hit print and sent the court documents to her printer.

"Let's go, girl," she leaned over and cupped Dot's head in her hands and then gave her a quick head scratch.

"We've had a good morning and deserve a sunny walk."

Pat's office answering machine blinked red and the time stamp indicated she had just missed a call. "Have we solved the case yet?" Syda's voice on her answering machine sounded slightly breathless.

"Are you so excited about the prospect of being a crime solver that you can't catch your breath?" Pat asked when she returned her friend's call.

"No. I recorded during a yoga workout. I know you are supposed to keep your breathing even, but I've never managed to master that during a warrior two pose. Well, have we?"

"Not yet, but we're hot on the trail."

"Really?" Syda asked incredulously.

"I found a connection between Angela Grinardi and Garryn Monteith. Let me get back to work and see if it looks stronger after some research."

"Keep me in the loop."

"Of course."

Pat had been thinking about that connection as she and Dot walked, especially since Angela was recently widowed. One piece of information she didn't have was how and why Leonardo Grinardi died, and she wanted to know.

She began her afternoon work by looking up year-old obituary notices in the Maryland town newspaper where Angela lived. She found Leonardo Grinardi's notice quickly. It confirmed that the three names listed in the

LexisNexis report were his children. The obituary stated he created beautiful glass art, but it didn't mention important placement of his work; and it said he was an art teacher in a local high school. So, Pat decided, he had never attained the prominence of his former business partner.

Pat read to the end of the notice hoping that a donations list might give her a clue as to why he died, but the only donation request was to a college fund for his daughter, and there was no wording such as "after a valiant fight against..." and no phraseology like "he died peacefully, surrounded by his loving family." The article ended with the name of the funeral home and date and time of a service. She was going to need a death certificate to find out how he died.

Pat logged on to the Maryland Vital Statistics homepage and clicked the certificates button. She immediately hit a wall. Maryland only issued death certificates to surviving family members and their authorized representatives and to funeral directors.

She surely wasn't the former. Her only recourse was the funeral director.

"Do you think Leonardo Grinardi has a long-lost aunt named Dot?' she asked her pet. "I could call and say I was representing you."

Dot slumped to the floor and buried her muzzle with her paws.

"Sometimes dogs are simply too honorable," she admonished. "I bet Wimsey wouldn't mind me using his identity nefariously."

She'd asked for various certificates before, but that was when she could declare herself a law librarian and part of a government entity. She was beginning to realize just how much harder everything would be now that she was the self-declared CEO of PIP Inc. It didn't matter. If she was going to succeed in her new career, she might have to split the difference between her and her pet's approach to the world. She dialed the number given in the obituary.

"Mortan's Funeral Home. Mr. Mortan speaking. How may I be of service?" a voice that oozed sympathy asked.

"Hello. I'm Pat Pirard in Santa Cruz, California. I'm hoping you will have some useful information in your file. I'm calling about one of your"—what did you call a body? A resident, a client, a guest?—"about Leonardo Grinardi, who died last May."

"Ahh, yes. I remember his family well; difficult situation, but they were so brave."

"Yes, the family is a remarkable one, which is in part why I'm calling." Pat took a deep breath and slipped into a full-on Wimsey. "His youngest brother was unable to attend the funeral. He's part of Doctors Without Borders and was on a mission at the time."

"Oh, bravo. An artist and a humanitarian in one family. I knew that family was special."

At first, Pat assumed the funeral director was vamping like she was, saying nice things without really remembering who Leonardo Grinardi was, buying time as he frantically searched the funeral home computer files to help jog his memory. But his response had been quick and seemed sincere. Now she wondered. Perhaps there was something else that made the service memorable to him. She took a chance.

"Sudden deaths like Mr. Grinardi's are always more difficult than most deaths are. Family members often find the circumstances hard to accept." She stopped speaking and left quiet space in case the funeral director might feel the need to fill the silence with some valuable information. Mr. Mortan did immediately.

"Indeed. Sudden deaths are always difficult. Accidents cause so much grief. Family members frequently say they can't believe what's happened and expect to see their loved one return and say their death was just a bad dream. But suicides are even worse. Survivors usually feel like they should have intervened in some way and saved their loved one."

Suicide. Leonardo Grinardi's death had been by his own hand. Her mouth formed an O and she almost sucked in enough air that Mr. Mortan could hear it over the phone.

"That's exactly how his brother feels. I think seeing what the informant told you about his brother might ease his pain, you know, reading all the wonderful things that were said about him for you to use in creating an obituary. Would it be possible for you to send me a copy of what was written?"

"Certainly."

"Oh, and by the way, would it be possible for you to send a copy of his death certificate, too? For closure. You can snail mail it to me at," Pat almost gave the Law

Library address from habit, but caught her mistake just in time and switched to her home address.

"I'll put copies in the mail today. There won't be any charge for them. I'm happy to do anything I can to ease a survivor's sense of loss."

"That's very kind of you, Mr. Mortan. Thank you so much."

The death certificate would list suicide as the cause of death, but it wouldn't say anything about why Leonardo Grinardi took his life. There was nothing definitive that said his death and Angela's plan were related, but the timing of Angela taking the class almost a year to the day after her husband's death and her promise were suggestive. It might have been just a feeling on her part, but Pat tied them together. She suspected somehow Leonardo's suicide and Garryn Monteith's death were connected.

Her first urge was to call Mark Bellows and let him know what she had discovered. As nice as it would have been to hear the sound of his voice and hope that he might ask to see her again, she fought her impulse. Unless she wanted to sound like an excitable amateur, she needed a lot more concrete information before she offered her theory to him.

Pat sat at her desk and drummed her foot. She badly wanted to call Angela Grinardi and ask her to confess. She looked at the phone number listed in Angela's LexisNexis report and picked up the phone, but the professional she aspired to be stopped her from dialing. She had to wait for the death certificate and think about what to say before she blurted out something that might warn Angela she was a suspect and give her time to concoct a believable cover story.

Besides, she had barely begun her investigation, and there were other potential suspects to consider, good distractions until she got her Angela ducks in a row. A prudent Pat called Syda instead of calling Angela.

"Hey, my detecting friend, I have a job for you."

"Oh goody. What do you want me to do and do I need to wear a fedora?"

"Hats are optional. I want you to call Suzanne Cummings—she's in the phonebook, so she won't think we're looking at her specially and researched her number—and set up a consoling lunch. You two could be commiserating about Garryn's loss, and I could just happen by, and you could invite me to join you."

"Why can't I make it lunch for three?"

"Because I don't think she'd agree to that."

"Oh, right, you were the competition. I forgot about that." Syda brightened. "A stealth lunch and meeting is great fodder for my research, too."

Syda was off before Pat could ask her what she meant.

"I've been thinking maybe my artistic career hasn't taken off because so far I haven't found my true calling. Maybe my muse will come to me if I create with words instead of paint or glass, or some of the other mediums I've tried.

"I'm thinking of becoming a writer. Possibly I'll do a noir story or maybe a first-person Sue Grafton–style private investigator kind of mystery. Lunch could make a great scene in either style book. I'll get right on that phone call. Should I ask her to meet me tomorrow for Mexican at Palomar?"

"Better make it Gayle's in Capitola. She lives near there, and I can be stopping by to pick up a pastry."

"Got it. I'll see you at oneish. I'll be the one in the blue fedora."

✳✳✳✳✳✳✳✳✳✳

Pat spied Syda and Suzanne Cummings the minute she walked through the main door at Gayle's Bakery, but she pretended she didn't see them. She took a number—even at one o'clock the line for service was still long—and leaned against the wall separating those waiting for bakery orders and those who had picked up their lunch and were eating in the sunny atrium behind the wall. After her order was filled, she would pretend to leave the eatery-cum-bakery via the atrium exit so she could accidently run into her quarry.

Pat's long wait for service meant she had a lot of time to peruse Gayle's array of temptations. When her number was called, she ordered a rustic baguette, half a dozen iced flower cookies, and a lemon sponge beehive cake filled with lemon curd and decorated with edible bees, many more baked goods than she intended to buy.

Her purchases turned out to be a perfect foil as she struggled to carry them all to the atrium exit: she knocked

Syda's hat off with the yard-long loaf of bread as she passed behind her.

"I'm so sorry! Oh, Syda, it's you," she sputtered with surprise recognition, "and Suzanne. Can I make up for my clumsiness by sharing some cookies with you? I overbought, but they looked so good."

Right on cue Syda said, "Cookies—of course you can share, can't she, Suzanne? Why don't you get a cup of coffee and join us?"

Pat put on one of her cheeriest smiles and deposited her baked goods on a vacant chair at the table. "I'd love to; I'll be right back."

Pat knew looks couldn't kill, but she could feel Suzanne's eye-daggers in her back all the way to the coffee counter.

As she carried her coffee back to the table, Pat noticed Syda had her hand on Suzanne Cummings's forearm and was leaning across the table speaking earnestly to her. Suzanne's eyes were downcast and she seemed about to cry.

Pat picked up Syda's last few words as she approached. "...she didn't encourage him."

Suzanne seemed so passive, sobbing in the bathroom, according to what she had told Syda, and avoiding any confrontation with Garryn, Pat, or anyone else she perceived as getting in the way with her imagined love relationship. But if she was a murderer, she had to have a planning, aggressive side, too. Pat made a split-second decision: she wasn't going to be nice to Suzanne

Cummings. She'd prod and see if Suzanne became pugnacious when pushed.

Pat put her coffee on the table, sat down, picked the bag of cookies up from the empty chair where they rested, and held the bag out to Suzanne. She smiled sweetly.

"Suzanne, I know you don't like me, but it's not my fault that Garryn Monteith found me attractive. He's not my type so I didn't encourage him, but even though I discouraged him, he still wasn't interested in you."

Suzanne blinked rapidly. "Excuse me, Syda. Thanks for inviting me to lunch, but I'm going to go now." She rose without acknowledging Pat and hurried to the atrium door.

"Oh, Pat," Syda chided, "That was cruel. Why did you say that to her?"

"I needed to see how she'd react. Now I feel like a high school mean girl. I'll write her an apology note, and after she's had a chance to think about what I say, I'll reach out to her and offer a more personal apology. I feel bad. She's obviously as meek as she seemed, but this is serious business. I had to know if she'd react like a wimp or a warrior. I had to see if she had a temper, if I thought she could get angry enough to kill."

"You could have asked me what I thought of her. We just had a long heart-to-heart over lunch. She was obsessed with Garryn, all right, but she would never have done anything to hurt him, let alone kill him. No way."

Syda munched on a cookie and Pat had a couple of sips of her coffee. They sat in silence, any enjoyment they might have had at playing detective at Gayle's was over.

They parted within a few minutes with a quick hug and headed out different doors, Syda via the atrium and Pat, toting her purchases, out the main door toward where she had parked her car.

She stopped abruptly as she got within sight of her beloved sunburst-yellow Mercedes. The windshield had a beginning spider web of cracked glass radiating out from a small hole on the driver's side just above the dashboard. She hadn't remembered a rock hitting the windshield as she drove. *How could...*

Suzanne Cummings drove past her slowly, smiled at her, and gave a little salute-like wave before she left the parking lot. She had committed a perfect crime. Pat would never be able to prove Suzanne had deliberately damaged her car, and yet it was clear that she had. And not only had Suzanne destroyed her windshield, she had waited for her so she could make sure Pat knew what had happened.

All Pat had done was say something unkind to Suzanne. What, she wondered, was the penalty for breaking her heart? Pat wondered if Garryn Monteith, gasping his final breath, had suspected Suzanne Cummings had killed him.

"Pat, you know the irony of this is that Super Glue applied to a windshield ping is said to stop it from spreading." Greg chuckled as he took down her statement.

"This was a weaponized poke, not a ping. I had to replace my windshield."

"You also know you're never going to get anywhere if you charge her, right?"

"I know. My evidence is all circumstantial. I didn't see her do anything to my car. That's why I'm telling you about this rather than filing a report with the Capitola police. I just want it on record somewhere, with someone, in case there's another incident."

"You think she's dangerous?"

"I don't know what to think. Yesterday I was convinced that another class member was a killer. Now I've completely changed my mind."

"Okay, I'll bury this in the file, but it'll be there like you want. Just be careful, will you, you and Syda. I love both of you and don't want anything to happen to either of you. A man is dead. This isn't just a great adventure for you to play at."

Was Suzanne Cummings dangerous? Greg's question was a good one. She was certainly jealous and vindictive, but Syda might be right about her not harming Garryn Monteith. So far Suzanne had taken out her rage on others and, according to Syda, only sobbed in the bathroom and tried harder to get his attention.

Pat made a quick call to Lillian Wentner. Joe answered the phone.

"Joe, you're a free man!" Pat said enthusiastically.

Joe sighed deeply. "For the time being at least. The judge set bail for me, saying even though the charge of first-degree murder was extremely serious, she respected my standing in the community and long history here, and didn't consider me a flight risk, although I had to turn in my passport and driver's license. She said the fact that I didn't have so much as a speeding ticket helped, too, so I didn't correct her misperception. I did get a speeding ticket about fifteen years ago."

"I think you lucked out with an able judge. Who's hearing your case?"

"Judge Blaine."

"She is good; wise, too, it sounds like. I had a quick question for you and Lillian about one of the students at the class. Could you check your records and see if Suzanne Cummings took any classes with you before?"

"I don't have to check anything to answer that question. She was a regular. Every time Garryn Monteith taught, she was here. She made an impression on me because she never looked the same from class to class. She'd be blonde, and then a brunette. Her weight fluctuated and so did her makeup and what she wore. Lillian and I talked about her. It was like every time we saw her she was trying to reinvent herself."

"Do you think she was changing her appearance because of Garryn? Maybe trying out different looks to see if any impressed him?"

"You'd have to ask Lillian about that. I don't know how she behaved during the classes. I only noticed that she always looked different—oh, and that she spent a lot of lunch breaks in the bathroom. I always wondered if there was something wrong with her health that she needed to spend so much time in there.

"Lillian's in town right now. Shall I ask her to give you a call when she gets back?"

"That's okay. I'll catch her next time I have more questions. Joe, I just thought of one more thing I wanted to ask you or Lillian: Did you ever get complaints about Suzanne from any of the people, women in particular, who took classes Garryn taught?"

"No. We've never had any problems during any of our classes—from her or anyone else."

Joe's observations were interesting. Suzanne's behavior certainly sounded odd, but it didn't raise any red flags. She might have hit a breaking point for some reason and become violent toward Garryn Monteith at the last class, but it seemed more probable that Syda was right, and that any hostile behavior Suzanne Cummings exhibited was directed against her perceived rivals rather than him.

Pat still fumed that Suzanne's rage had been aimed at her dream car, but she was less certain about Suzanne as a murderer than she had been before talking to Joe.

That meant it was back to work looking at suspects. Pat picked up Kandi Crusher's file and scanned it for anything noteworthy. She didn't find anything. Kandi appeared to be what Syda would have called a "good girl." She had no violations, no bankruptcies, no liens or judgments filed against her, and she hadn't filed any against anyone else.

The only reason Pat was even looking at her file was because Kandi, like Angela Grinardi, had made a curious comment during the class. Pat recalled she started talking to Kandi because they were both hanging back from the adoring throng at lunch the second day of instruction. If she remembered correctly, Kandi labeled Garryn Monteith self-aggrandizing and implied his class wasn't worth what it cost. And yet, she said she planned to get a lot out of the class the next day. It wasn't much as suspicious statements went, but it resonated with her.

Had she known what the future held, Pat might have delved more deeply into what Kandi meant by that, but there weren't any dead bodies lying around when Kandi made her comment, and that thread of conversation ended as soon as Kandi told her that her full name was Kandi Crusher.

Pat smiled as she remembered how she had suggested ways Kandi could get away from that moniker.

*That moniker.*

As she thought about it, Pat developed that unsettled feeling that comes when remembrance is there, but the specifics of it are just out of reach. She tried to recall what it was about Kandi's name that was causing her uneasiness. It troubled her that the cause was close in her mind and yet remained elusive.

She flipped to the first page of the LexisNexis report and reread Kandi's biographical information: *Kandi Mann Crusher, female.* That was as far as she needed to go before the synapse closed. She scanned Kandi's relative connections again: George Harold Crusher, Samuel Mann Crusher, Cindi Ann Mann Crusher, Henry David Crusher, Maryanne Penelope Mann Crusher Frieberg, Peter Mann Frieberg. There were other names, but she had found what she needed.

Pat remembered Kandi's story about her husband, George Crusher, having a locker above her in high school. George was her husband. Samuel and Cindi—spelling names with an *i* rather than a *y* seemed to be a family thing with the Crushers, as was including their mother's maiden name—Mann—in children's names. Henry David Crusher's name was followed by the triangle with an exclamation point that indicated he was deceased. He was probably Kandi's father. And Maryanne Penelope Mann Crusher Frieberg would be her remarried mother who produced a son with her second husband. That would make Peter Mann Frieberg, whose information was also preceded by a triangle with an exclamation point, Kandi's half-brother.

His was the name Pat recalled seeing somewhere. She grabbed Garryn Monteith's file and looked at his legal section. Peter Mann Frieberg was listed as both a litigant and a business associate.

Six years ago Peter Frieberg had sued Garryn Monteith for $156,000, but the case had been dismissed. She wanted to find out what the suit was about and why it had failed.

Probably because she liked her, Pat found it hard to make Kandi a murder suspect. A six-year-old alleged debt between Garryn Monteith and Kandi's half-brother couldn't be a motive for murder, could it? Hardly. And yet, in her work for local attorneys, she'd seen cases when people were killed because of less money than that. Her logical mind told her not to believe in someone's innocence just because she liked them.

There was something else Pat hadn't pursued with Kandi: she remembered Kandi had said something about Lillian Wentner being someone else Garryn Monteith used when it was convenient. She wanted to know more about that, too.

Looking at Lillian's contacts list, she saw that Kandi lived on the coast about fifteen miles south of San Francisco in the community of Pacifica, a mere hour's drive up Highway 1 from Santa Cruz.

She and Kandi had established some rapport during the class. She could contact Kandi, share the latest gossip about Joe's arrest, ask her to expand what she said about Garryn and Lillian, and do all of that without raising suspicion that she was investigating Kandi because of the connection between Peter Frieberg and Garryn Monteith. All she needed was a good reason to be passing through Pacifica so she'd have an innocent excuse for a visit.

Pat looked at Dot who was in her usual position by the Wimsey chair and smiled slyly. She entered "Dalmatian breeders Bay Area" in her computer and hoped for a suitable outcome. She was rewarded with exactly what she wanted—something better than she hoped, actually—when she saw there was a Dalmatian breeder in Pacifica.

"Dot, how would you like to go visit a breeder? Maybe meet a nice guy dog with the idea in mind that you want to become a mommy?"

Dot perked up at the sound of her name and began wagging her tail vigorously. She followed Pat's words so closely that it was hard to think she didn't understand them.

"We won't tell Kandi that you've been spayed. We'll keep that just between us girls."

Pat pulled up the website for Gallard's Hot 2 Spot Dalmatians and familiarized herself with it enough that her interest in the breeder could sound genuine if Kandi questioned her about it.

Kandi's phone number was on the contact sheet Lillian had given her. The phone rang five times after she dialed before it went to answering mode. She hurriedly came up with something to say that would entice Kandi to return her call, but as it turned out, she didn't need to use it. All she got out was, "Hi Kandi. This is Pat Pirard from the glass class," when a live female voice said, "Pat," enthusiastically.

"Kandi?"

"Yes. I was here, but screening. This week's robocalls are all about knee braces, and I'm sick to death of them. I hope if they keep getting an answering machine, they'll give up and leave me alone." She laughed lightly after her explanation. "What's up?"

"Have you heard about Joe Wentner?

"No. Should I know something about him?" Pat detected a hint of excitement in Kandi's voice. Good gossip was definitely a currency Kandi accepted.

"He's been arrested and charged with murdering Garryn Monteith."

Pat heard a sharp inhalation of air, clear even over the phone. "That's ridiculous. We all saw Garryn die; he had a heart attack."

"That's what everyone thought until they did an autopsy on him. It turns out he was murdered."

"Well, I did think it was unlikely that he had a heart attack, considering that he didn't have a heart, but murder? And Joe? He's such a nice man. Do you think he could have killed Garryn?"

"I'll tell you all about it if you'll meet me for lunch. I've been putting off spaying my Dalmatian, Dot. I read somewhere it's a good thing to let females have a litter of pups before they are spayed, and I think she's getting ready to come into season soon, so I want to find her a suitable stud. There's a breeder in Pacifica who has a dog that sounds perfect. Dot and I are going to take a ride up the coast and see what she thinks of him. We could meet somewhere and have lunch."

"Pacifica isn't particularly dog friendly and I love dogs. Why don't you and Dot come to my house for lunch? Her temperament is good, isn't it? She wouldn't menace my Chihuahua, would she?"

"Dot lives with a cat. Need I say more?"

Kandi snorted her amusement. "How about the day after tomorrow?"

❊❊❊❊❊❊❊❊❊❊

Kandi's house was back far enough from the coast and high enough in the hills that swept away from the ocean that it sat above Pacifica's shrouding fog. On a clear day it would have offered an ocean view, but today sun was all it could boast.

Pat parked and confirmed the blue house with crisp white trim was the one she sought. She snapped Dot's collar onto her leash and got out of the car. Dot followed her in a bound over the driver's seat and out the door.

As they started to the house's entry door, it opened and Kandi met them at the front lawn. She dropped to her knees and hugged Dot. "Aren't you a beauty? Aren't you a good dog?" she crooned.

Dot fell in love with Kandi instantly. Her tail, too expressive for a simple side to side wag, worked like a propeller. Pat put great store in her dog's opinion of people. Kandi got the Dot Seal of Approval; Pat felt sure that she couldn't be a murderer.

"Come in, come in, both of you," Kandi invited as she got up. She didn't hug Pat.

A quivering Chihuahua with a heavily gray muzzle greeted them as soon as they stepped inside. "Dot, meet Cheetah. Cheetah, this is Dot, and her person, Pat. No barking or growling. They're friends."

Kandi slid open a back door to the garden and Cheetah led Dot outside amid doggie get-to-know-you sniffing. "They can play while we have lunch and talk."

They climbed the short flight of stairs from the entry to the entertaining portion of the split-level house where Kandi had sandwiches, fruit salad, and cookies laid out for lunch.

"I'm no master de la cuisine like Joe," Kandi blended Spanish and French as she described her cooking abilities, "but I do make a good avocado and cheese sandwich. And speaking of Joe, what's going on? You said he was arrested."

"He was. He's out on bail and I've been hired by his attorney to try and absolve him of murder." Pat produced one of her newly minted PIP Inc. cards and handed it to Kandi."

"Get out! You're a private investigator?"

"New private investigator. This is my first case."

"I've always thought it would be fun to be a private investigator," Kandi grinned. "Let me know how it goes, will you? But what about Joe? Why do they think he killed Garryn Monteith? Did Lillian and Garryn's same-time-next-year arrangement finally get to him?"

Pat got Kandi's reference, but she looked puzzled and tilted her head to encourage more of an explanation. "What kind of arrangement is that?"

"Remember the Alan Alda movie, *Same Time Next Year*, where this couple were both happily married to other people, but got together once a year for a couple of days in Mendocino for a little…" Kandi pointed her index fingers upward and swirled them as she raised her eyebrows "…um-mum. Well, Lillian and Garryn…"

"Nooo." Pat drew out the word for a gossipy and dramatic effect. "Are you sure?"

"Absolutely. My brother was in business with Garryn for years. Garryn would come back from Santa Cruz and, well, let's just say he wasn't into the gentlemanly don't-kiss-and-tell rule."

"And you think Joe knew about it?" Pat continued in her best scandalized tone.

"Duh; he must have. Joe doesn't seem like an oblivious dummy to me. Imagine putting up with that year after year. I sure couldn't have put up with it if George was getting some on the side on a regular basis. You didn't say how Garryn was killed. How did he die?"

"Cyanide poisoning," Pat said matter-of-factly.

"So the police think Joe had finally had enough and slipped cyanide into Garryn's food?"

"That's what they thought, but now it looks like he inhaled cyanide when he opened the kiln door."

"There's not enough cyanide in the Super Glue we used

to hold our pieces in place before firing to hurt anyone."

Pat was startled that Kandi knew about cyanide in Super Glue, but hoped her surprise hadn't been obvious. "No there's not, but if several tubes of Super Glue were in the kiln, there would be enough cyanide in them to prove lethal, at least for the person who opened the kiln."

Kandi sucked in her cheeks in momentary contemplation. "Cool. Couldn't have happened to a more deserving guy. He hurt a lot of people in his career climb, or should I say his claw to the top." She took a decisive bite of her sandwich.

"You said your brother worked for Garryn…"

"He didn't 'work for Garryn.' They were business partners. They started their glass company in California back in the day and were doing okay—no spectacular success, though—until Garryn 'forgot' to pay state taxes and the IRS. Peter had given Garryn his share of the money owed, too. The IRS came after them, and my brother wound up paying back taxes and fines to get them out of trouble."

"If Garryn was the one who messed up, why didn't your brother make him pay the taxes and fines?"

"Garryn? The great artist? He convinced my brother that he couldn't understand complicated things like filing a proper tax return. He said if Peter would take care of the IRS, he'd pay him back and pay the California taxes, which were a lot less.

"My brother, trusting idiot, agreed. I don't think the California taxes got paid completely, because the next thing my brother knew, Garryn said they should move their company to Florida. In a hurry. My brother went along again. At least Garryn must have paid something, because the state never came after Peter. Or maybe it was the move that saved them." Kandi shrugged her shoulders.

"Why do I think Garryn never repaid your brother?" Pat asked.

"Because you are a skilled private investigator," Kandi laughed. "No, he never did. He borrowed more money from Peter, and my brother often was working for free to help them stay in business. Then Garryn got a commission from some rich guy in Dubai and became the darling of the high-roller crowd. That's when he severed all ties with my brother and moved 'his' company to New York."

"So Garryn never repaid your brother what he owed him?"

"Oh, he gave him ten grand, but he was into Peter for a lot more than that. My brother sued him, but he didn't win. Then my baby brother, nice guy, no balls, sucked it up and let it go. He passed away a couple of years ago, so Garryn got away with stealing from him. I should have let it go, too, but it ate at me. That's why I took the class. I was really looking forward to making Garryn look foolish, but I didn't even get to do that."

"What a terrible thing to do to a partner and friend." Pat didn't have to muster any fake outrage for her statement.

"He treated my brother bad, but he did worse things to other people. He stole his stem-attachment method from another guy he knew."

"The stem system is a big deal, isn't it?"

"It is. It's Garryn's bread-and-butter teaser to fill classes, but I gather from my brother that it's what enables—enabled," Kandi smiled as she corrected herself, "Garryn to build the giant glass flowers that became his trademark and led to his success.

"My brother said some other guy who partnered with Garryn before he did was the real inventor of Garryn's super system. Evidently he was excited about what he developed and showed it to Garryn. Garryn convinced the poor guy that he should patent his system, offered to help him fill out the paperwork to do it, and said he'd turn everything in to the patent office. He did, all right, but not until after he substituted his name as inventor. Nice, huh? If I was the poor schmuck who got cheated out of my patent, I would have killed him."

Dot busied herself with licking her fur to remove the green grass stains that covered her after her romp in Kandi's backyard. From her appearance, it looked like Cheetah was the alpha dog in their play time and Dot had spent a lot of time submissively on her back on the lawn.

It was good that Dot was occupied as they drove back to Santa Cruz. Pat was so deep in thought about what Kandi told her during lunch that she was barely concentrating on driving, and she had no focus left over for her dog.

Kandi was open about what happened to her brother and never mentioned him inciting revenge. Those facts argued against Kandi being Garryn Monteith's killer. But Kandi knew about cyanide in Super Glue. There was no aha moment for her; she knew. If her motive was weak, her opportunity wasn't. Kandi could easily have come prepared with what she needed to kill and a plan about how to do it ready for execution. Since Pat wanted Kandi to be innocent, that was worrisome.

Even more troubling was what Kandi said about Lillian and Garryn's regular get-togethers. If Joe knew about their biannual assignations, a jury might be persuaded his years of tolerance meant he had given his blessing to the arrangement and had no motive for murder. But suppose, like Kandi speculated, he'd finally had enough, finally snapped. Worse still, suppose he hadn't known about their ongoing flings. If he just found out about them...she didn't want to think about what that meant.

Pat arrived home with a clean white dog to see a postal truck turning right at the end of her block, its driver having finished his deliveries on her street. She pulled her car into her garage and returned to the curb to open her mailbox. A packet with a Maryland return address was stuffed inside. Pat opened it as she walked to her front door with a leashless Dot following her.

She tossed her other mail on the coffee table, flopped on her sofa, and pulled the contents out of the packet. There were notes from the family about Leonardo Grinardi—nothing enlightening, just the usual about how much he was loved and respected used to create a newspaper obituary—and the death certificate.

Cause of death was listed as *Acute overdose of self-*

*administered Pentobarbital.* That made it clear Leonardo Grinardi had taken his own life. In the next section, where underlying conditions were listed, was the phrase *amyotrophic lateral sclerosis.* He had ALS, Lou Gehrig's Disease.

While such information didn't mean Angela Grinardi was no longer a suspect, it removed the strong motive to kill that she would have had if her husband ended his life because he was, for example, depressed at not being recognized for his singular invention or some other reason related to Garryn Monteith.

So Angela moved down her suspects list and Kandi and Joe moved up a notch.

Pat decided another consultation with Mark Bellows was warranted. She went to her closet and searched for an outfit that was even more seductive than her green dress. When she had selected a soft blue cashmere sweater with a boat neck that let it fall off a shoulder if she wanted it to, she called him.

"My suspects list is firming up, but I don't like where it's heading, and I don't think you will, either."

Pat sat in Mark Bellows's plush law office to deliver her update. She was dressed in a bright yellow skirt and similarly colored stilettos, a sensible if slightly flirty peplum jacket, and a leopard-print scarf that matched her briefcase and was loosely tied around her neck.

The meeting was already a disappointment—there was no cashmere sweater, no dinner and drinks—and it was destined to get worse as she delivered bad news.

"Tell me straight. It's only a matter of time before the District Attorney discovers the basic facts, too. I need your interpretation of them if I'm going to help my client."

Pat didn't have to open her briefcase and retrieve notes; she already knew what she was going to say.

"Angela Grinardi's late husband was the inventor of Garryn Monteith's glass attachment system. Monteith tricked him and stole the patent. Leonardo Grinardi committed suicide about a year ago, leaving his family asking for contributions to his daughter's college expenses, so I would say not terribly well off."

"I thought you said I wasn't going to like your results?

With what you've just told me, I could build a narrative for reasonable doubt."

"He had ALS."

"Oh."

Pat nodded sympathetically.

"Garryn Monteith may have been a scoundrel and a thief, but what he did to Leonardo Grinardi and his family happened years ago. I think Angela wanted to cause a stir and embarrass Garryn in front of his class, but you'd have a hard time convincing a jury she was seeking revenge and might be a murderer."

"Okay," Mark sighed. "We won't pursue that route anymore. What about our local Suzanne Cummings?"

"She's obsessive, malicious, and in my opinion, nuts."

Mark Bellows leaned back in his leather executive chair with a quizzical look on his face. "She sounds perfect. Tell me more."

"She's taken many of Garryn Monteith's classes at the Glass House. Joe says she was a regular, and who knows where else she might have followed Garryn. It seems she's obsessed with trying to rekindle the star pupil thing— which apparently is a euphemism for a romantic liaison during a class—that they had previously. Garryn was no longer interested in her, and she was clearly distraught about that."

"She sounds like a stalker, and stalkers have been known to kill the object of their stalking. Suzanne Cummings sounds promising as a murder suspect."

"I thought so, too, especially after she broke my

windshield in the parking lot at Gayle's Bakery when I shook her up by reminding her that Garryn hit on me during the glass class."

"What?" Mark asked incredulously. "Did you file a police report? If you did, I could really make a case that she's prone to violence."

"I did report her, sort of. I told Deputy Sherriff Greg Gonzales, who's a friend of mine, what happened. He took notes, but I didn't make an official report because I didn't see her do it. Even though I know she did, my evidence would sound speculative and could be taken apart by any merely adequate DA."

Mark's enthusiasm didn't wane. "Do you have anything else on her that I can use? If you can find any other instances of aggressive behavior on her part, well, coupled with her provable stalking behavior, I could still use what she did to your car to make a strong case against her."

"I'll see if I can find anything else she's done." Pat's lack of enthusiasm was conspicuous.

Mark noticed and prompted her. "What else do you already have that's not going to be helpful?" he asked.

"Suzanne Cummings spent long periods of time in the bathroom during lunch breaks. I thought she could easily have slipped out and put Super Glue tubes in the kiln while everyone assumed she was still in the bathroom."

"That's perfect. That screams motive and opportunity."

Pat shook her head. "Joe said that she always sequestered herself after the morning session because Garryn always ignored her. He said she'd have a good cry and then try to make herself look good, and my friend Syda, who was also at the class, confirms that. Suzanne Cummings probably was in the bathroom sobbing during the whole lunch break and not sneaking out to kill Garryn Monteith, so there goes opportunity."

"So you're saying she's a stalker capable of violence toward perceived competitors, but you don't think she went after her love interest?"

"Right now, I think that's the case."

"Who's up next?" Mark asked.

"Kandi Crusher. I found out that her brother was also swindled by Garryn Monteith. She knew all about cyanide in Super Glue, and she definitely told me she didn't like Garryn. That's the problem with her as a suspect. She was the one who brought up what happened to her brother and how she felt about it. She was open about her dislike of the man and her plan to embarrass him in front of the class. I don't think she'd tell me what she did if she killed him. She'd be quiet or have another story ready to tell. I just don't see her as the killer."

"You like her, don't you?"

"So does my dog."

Pat instantly wished she could take back her last words, but Mark began laughing with her like she'd made a joke, not at her like she was a flake. Hopefully that meant she hadn't damaged the professional image she was intent on projecting.

She recrossed her legs and began speaking again, going for a fresh start.

"Now we get into the bad news part. Kandi told me Lillian Wentner and Garryn Monteith had been involved intermittently for a long time. She quoted her brother's firsthand knowledge that Lillian and Garryn got together every time he taught a class at the glass studio. She thought Joe had to know about their relationship and was okay with it.

"I immediately thought: Suppose he didn't know and just found out, or suppose he simply got fed up with them carrying on right under his nose?"

"Major motive for murder," Mark said like a man who had just lost all hope. "You believe her?"

"I do, but it doesn't matter what I think. Her brother died a couple of years ago, so he can't testify—"

Mark talked over her, "—Which makes what Kandi Crusher says hearsay."

"Exactly."

"Thank God," Mark mumbled. He leaned his head forward, dropping it into his hand, and began scratching it just above the hairline.

"I'll quiz Joe," he sighed. "You take another look at Suzanne Cummings. What a mess."

Pat had her marching orders. She rose and started to leave. Just as she reached for the handle on Mark's office door, he called after her.

"Oh, Pat? Just to make things clear, this was a business meeting. I asked you to come to my office for a professional work matter. That way, the next time I ask you out to dinner, you'll know that we're on a date and not at work."

He flashed a disarmingly broad smile at her, and she thought she might have gotten some color in her cheeks.

"Good to know," she smiled back before she left his office.

❋❋❋❋❋❋❋❋❋❋

Pat was relieved that her phone call the next morning reached Lillian instead of Joe. Now that she knew what she did about Lillian's relationship with Garryn Monteith, it was going to be hard enough to carry on a nothing's-up conversation with Lillian. She wasn't sure she could pull it off with Joe, regardless of how many college drama classes she'd taken.

"Good morning, Lillian. How are you holding up at the Glass House?"

"Hanging on by our fingernails, although we have a class scheduled next week—if we have anyone willing to come by then. We've already had almost half the students cancel. It's amazing how far word about murder spreads and how quickly it moves. At least it's a class I'm teaching, so we don't have to worry about the instructor quitting."

Lillian tried to end her statement with a lighthearted little laugh, but it failed. Pat responded similarly with the same result.

"Lillian, I have a favor to ask."

"Anything, especially if it will help Joe."

"I'm hoping it will. Joe mentioned Suzanne Cummings was a regular. I need you to check your records and find classes Garryn Monteith taught where Suzanne Cummings attended. Can you do that?"

"It should be easy. In addition to doing all the cooking for the classes, Joe keeps detailed records. I'm useless with computers, but he should be able to find that information in a flash."

"If he finds other classes she attended, I'm going to need class list contact information for students in those classes, too."

"I don't think it will be hard for Joe to do an additional search. Do you want him to email the results to you, or do you want to pick them up?"

"I'll come to you. I want to have a private talk with you anyway, so perhaps we could get together when Joe is doing something else?" Pat questioned.

"Joe has a phone conference with Mark Bellows at 11:00 this morning. Would that work for you?

"I'll see you then."

The day was balmy and bright with sunshine, and Pat decided it was time to christen her convertible for what it was. She drove with the top down and neatly folded in the trunk for the first time. There was nothing Dot liked better than a ride in Pat's car; a top-down adventure would make her week. Dot was one happy Dalmatian as they drove toward Bonny Doon. She sat upright in the passenger seat, letting the wind blow her ears back gently, her mouth open and filled with air. Pat was sure she was smiling.

"You'll have to stay in the car when we get to the Glass House. I don't know how they feel about dogs, and you can't run around outside. I know you: you'll see a squirrel and be gone."

When they reached the Wentners' house, Pat parked under trees for shade, pushed the button to put up the convertible top, and cracked her window so Dot would be comfortable. "You stay here; I won't be long."

Lillian greeted Pat at the front door when she knocked. "Come in. I have Joe's printout ready for you, but you said you wanted to talk to me?"

"I do," Pat said as she settled into a cushy seat in the living room. "I want to know about Suzanne Cummings's behavior in classes taught by Garryn Monteith. Were you in the studio whenever Garryn taught, like you were when I took the class?"

"That's right. I was always in the studio as Garryn's unofficial assistant."

"Garryn seemed, um, willing to give me some private lessons during the class."

Lillian straightened up until her seated posture was starched.

"Suzanne Cummings, who was seated next to me and had been friendly until Garryn made his offer, wouldn't have anything to do with me after that. What I'm wondering is, would you have noticed who Garryn Monteith was especially interested in at other classes and what Suzanne Cummings's reaction was to them?"

"I noticed how Garryn tried to treat you at the class, but I can't say I noticed Suzanne Cummings having any unusual reaction to it."

"What about at other classes?"

"Garryn would sometimes talk to me after class and say he noticed a student who seemed especially talented, but I'm unaware that he offered any of them special help. I never noticed Suzanne Cummings acting oddly toward any of the other students."

Lillian hadn't exactly answered her question, and for a minute, Pat thought she hadn't been clear enough about what she wanted to know. She was about to clarify her question when she instead chose to go in a different direction.

"Did Garryn talk to you about me?"

"No," Lillian said dismissively. "We were especially busy during your class because it was larger than usual, and we didn't have a chance to speak privately about you or anything else. And then...then the class ended differently than it usually did."

Their conversation was interrupted by loud barking. Pat recognized the bark at once. She jumped up and rushed to the window. The roof on her car was slowly retracting into the trunk. Dot bounced friskily outside the car and barked at it urgently.

Within seconds, Pat was out the front door, running full speed along the porch toward the stairs, heading for the commotion.

"Dot! Sit! Sit!" she yelled. "Sit right now or I'll never

take you for a ride again."

Pat bounded down the front stairs, past the decorative flower garden, and over the lawn to her dog, who had obeyed immediately, but seemed ready to change her mind at any moment.

Was it possible Dot had figured out which button to push to turn her new car into a convertible? Pat was afraid the answer was yes, she had. The only question was, had Dot done it accidently or was she capable of doing it deliberately?

Lillian followed Pat to the car at a much slower pace, the printouts of information Pat requested in her arms. She obviously thought what had happened was funny, and she was laughing loudly as she followed Pat.

"You have quite a trickster for a dog," Lillian continued laughing.

"Dot is a notorious refrigerator door opener," an exasperated Pat offered. "I've convinced her to stay out of mine, but I met my next-door neighbors the day they were moving in after retrieving her and the string of sausages she had stolen from their refrigerator. They left their front door open as they unloaded boxes and furniture, and she couldn't resist going inside and helping herself."

Lillian's laughter tinkled with delight.

Pat reached into her car, pushed the convertible button, and reversed the car-top's direction. Once she was sure her dog couldn't squeeze out through the not-quite-secure roof, she pushed Dot back into the car.

"I think I have what I need," Pat said as she took the

papers from Lillian. "I'll say thanks for your answers and head home. It looks like I have an afternoon of dog training in front of me."

Pat got an early start the next morning matching up the names and phone numbers from classes Garryn Monteith taught at the Glass House with women who had attended them. The work was tedious; the results shocked her. *My gosh, she's been stalking him for at least eight years.* Suzanne Cummings might have been following Garryn Monteith for even longer, she realized, but that was as far back as the Wentners' records went.

Over the years, an average of fourteen women attended each class that Suzanne Cummings attended: 168 names. Subtracting the 16 for the class she and Syda attended brought the number of names down to 152. She subtracted Suzanne Cummings's name twelve times, since she wasn't going to call Suzanne and ask her about her behavior, and removed duplicate entries of the women who had attended more than one class. She was left with 117 names. She sighed, poured herself a mug of coffee, and set to work, dialing women from classes in reverse order.

By 2:30, when her stomach insisted she take a break, she had reached eighty-three women and discovered twenty-two of the phone numbers were no longer in service. That left her a dozen numbers to dial or redial so that she could ask them the same question: Do you remember a woman named Suzanne Cummings in the class you took? Few did. She scratched those who didn't remember Suzanne off her list, reasoning if she hadn't made a lasting impression on them, she hadn't threatened them.

Of those who did remember her, Pat asked a good open-ended question: What do you remember about her? Most remembered her as a tablemate; none of their responses led to her final question: What did she do to you?

At 4:30 she was hoarse and frustrated. *What a useless exercise.* Pat wanted to stop calling, but she wasn't a quitter. She was determined that, at her next report, she could honestly tell Mark she had tried heroically to get another witness to Suzanne Cummings's violent behavior, but that none existed, at least among those who attended class at the Glass House.

Pat spent the rest of the afternoon researching Garryn Monteith online to see where he most often taught besides the Glass House. The list was long. He taught an average of six classes a year elsewhere and seemed to repeat in only a couple of locations. She called as many class locations as she could find. When she told the venue's owners what had happened to him, most were willing to look for the name Suzanne Cummings in their contact lists. When she got a hit, she asked for names and phone numbers of students who shared a class with her.

Pat's email was loaded with dozens more names and phone numbers by the time she completed her Glass House calls in the early evening.

She couldn't face another day like she had just had. She needed help and knew where to ask for it.

"Syda, are you creating?" Pat asked when her friend answered her phone.

"I am. It turns out that I'm a terrific writer. Let me read my opening lines to you.

*Private detective Rowdy Dick looked down at the body that washed up on shore with crabs clinging to it and chewing on the flesh on its face. He turned to his stacked red-haired secretary and said, "Whew, thank God it's only crabs eating her. If it was lobsters, I don't know what I'd do, Babe. I could never eat one again.*

"Good, isn't it?"

Pat bit her lip. "It's interesting. I'm not sure about the PI's name, though.

"It's just a working name. I have other ideas for his name, too."

"Good. I was hoping you'd help me do a really boring job, but it sounds like you're busy."

"No, no," Syda said quickly. "Writing is exhausting. And after that really strong opening, I'm experiencing writer's block. I could use a break. What do you want me to do?"

"Help me make phone calls."

"What kind of phone calls?"

"Calls to women Suzanne Cummings might have threatened."

"After what she did to your darling car, I'm in. Come to me. We can work in my kitchen."

✻✻✻✻✻✻✻✻✻✻

The first words out of Syda's mouth when she opened her kitchen door for Pat the next morning were a dismayed, "Oh, gee. Jeans and a baggy pink tee-shirt; that's what you're wearing?"

"Since when do you care if I get comfortable for a hard day's work?" Pat protested.

"I usually don't. It's just that...if you at least tucked in the tee-shirt, I have a nice belt you could borrow. Or you could tuck in the front, French style. That would help. There's no help for your flats, though. They look like they're ten years old."

"That's because they are ten years old."

Syda shook her head. "I can't help with those. Your feet are bigger than mine, so I can't loan you a pair of decent shoes."

"You don't look that fancy this morning yourself, Syda."

"I know," Syda blurted out, "but I'm not trying to impress anyone."

"Neither am I," Pat parried. "Syda?"

"Well, it's possible that Greg forgot to take something with him this morning and he's going to swing by to pick it up, and he'll be here around coffee-break time, and so he might as well come in and have coffee here, and it would be rude to leave his partner in the patrol car, and so he might come in, too, and..."

Pat's eyes were closed by the time Syda got to the end of her explanation, and she heaved an exaggerated sigh.

"It's your fault," Syda chastised. "You've been making it impossible for Greg and me to introduce you to his partner. You can't blame me for getting frustrated and jumping on the only chance I saw of having you two meet. They'll be here any minute. Tuck," Syda mimed. "Tuck."

Pat had just divided up the list, explained how to order questions, and called one woman so Syda could hear what she said, when Greg burst into the room and gave Syda a kiss.

"Hey, Pat. I didn't know you were going to be here," Greg said in a voice Pat thought was rather high for him. He strung his words together unnaturally, with even spaces between them. "I don't know how I could have forgotten my book, but as long as I'm here now and it's break time, how about we join you for a cup of coffee? This is my partner, at least for a couple more days, Tim Lindsey. Tim, you know my wife, and this is her best friend, Pat."

"Syda, Pat," Tim said. "Actually, Pat and I already met. I interviewed her about the Garryn Monteith murder case."

Pat smiled at him and then at Syda. "Yes, he did."

From the bemused expression on Tim Lindsey's face, Pat thought he had been blindsided by the setup just like she had.

"Let's have coffee. I just made a big pot for Pat and me," Syda invited. "Coincidently, we are working on something related to that murder today."

Tim didn't need an invitation. He sat down next to Pat.

131

"Oh yeah? What are you doing?"

"Pat had a run-in with one of the women in the class," Syda started.

"Her behavior was odd," Pat explained, "and we're trying to find out if it was an anomaly or if she has a history of doing similar things."

Tim looked puzzled. "Why are you doing that?"

"I've been hired by Mark Bellows, Joe Wentner's attorney, to help him defend Joe," Pat said.

Syda piped up with, "Pat's a private investigator."

"Are you now?" Tim grinned.

"Trying to be," Pat answered.

"Did I give you my card before?" Tim reached in his jacket pocket, produced his sheriff's contact card, and handed it to Pat. "If you come up with anything the Sheriff's Department should know, now that you're a private investigator, will you give me a call?"

Greg started to say, "Or you could tell me," before Syda kicked him under the table.

After Greg and his partner finished their coffee and returned to their patrol car, Syda pounced. "What do you think? Isn't he nice?"

Pat tried for a Mona Lisa smile. She wasn't about to let Syda know her second impression of Tim Lindsey matched her first impression of him: that he was cute and intelligent, traits that made him an attractive man. The fact that he was comfortable in his skin didn't hurt either.

"He is. Now let's get to work."

Syda was the first to get to the third question. "What did she do to you?" she asked as she made frantic hand motions to Pat, encouraging her to listen in.

"Nothing physical, exactly," the woman said. "Nothing like boiling my rabbit in a pot or anything like that. She sent me a letter telling me something bad was going to happen to me if I didn't leave Garryn Monteith alone."

Pat hurriedly turned over the phone-and-name list they were using and scribbled a question on it for Syda to ask. "How do you know the letter was from her?"

"She signed it."

Pat soundlessly opened her mouth.

"Could I put you on speaker so my associate can hear what you're saying, too? And ask you a question?" Syda asked.

"Sure."

"Hi, I'm Pat Pirard. Do you still have the letter?"

"No, I got rid of it. It creeped me out reading it; I wasn't about to save it."

"Was that the only contact she had with you after the class?"

"Yeah. What she wrote made me uncomfortable, but nothing came of it, unless you count the fact that I never took another class taught by Garryn Monteith, even though I wanted to."

"I apologize for having to ask this, but did you have any sort of relationship with Garryn Monteith outside of class?"

There was a long silence before the line went dead.

"I'll take that as a yes," Pat said.

A pattern emerged as Syda and Pat worked their way through the call lists. Garryn Monteith did have some connection with a woman in almost all the classes he taught. Most labeled what happened between them as a mere flirtation, but some of the pauses and over-explaining Pat heard made her think his reputation as a philanderer was earned.

Women who admitted to receiving any sort of special attention from him, even when they insisted what happened between them was innocent, were frequently harassed, usually in ways that could be written off as accidents or coincidences.

Glass pieces would be accidently knocked off of a worktable and shattered. Air might be let out of tires. The spider poke of a windshield happened to one of the women just like it had to Pat, but the woman attributed it to bad luck and a rock on the road, even though she didn't remember anything hitting her windshield as she drove to class.

Other than the beginner's-luck hit Syda had in the morning, none of the women had received a clear threat like a letter from Suzanne Cummings, although a couple of them said she made passing comments, which they remembered because what she said made them uneasy.

One woman, whose finished work was shattered, said Suzanne consoled her and then said, "It's too bad what happened to your piece, but it's not like someone broke into your gallery and smashed everything in it." She said she had hardly spoken to Suzanne Cummings during the class and wondered at the time how she could have known about her owning a glass gallery.

One woman, who discovered her tires were flat, told Pat that Suzanne had flitted by her and said something about it being good it happened where she could call AAA, because if it happened on some of the roads she drove to get home, she'd be stuck.

The woman insisted she hadn't even spoken to Suzanne Cummings during the class and certainly had never mentioned that she lived a couple of miles up a twisting road in the hills outside Denver where cell coverage was sparse. She felt strongly that Suzanne Cummings could only have known where she lived if she had followed her home. When pressed, the woman admitted that Garryn Monteith had been invited to her house.

"I'm so frustrated," Pat said. "It's just like Suzanne's attack on my car. I know she did it, but it's a feeling I have, not anything I can prove. I doubt anything we've discovered will help Mark get Joe exonerated."

"You should call Tim. I bet he'll be able to help."

"You just want me to call Tim."

"Of course I do. I think you two have real chemistry, but I meant call him like the deputy sheriff he is. The Sheriff's Department is working the case, and they can do follow-ups and have more resources than we do."

"How can you reach the conclusion that we have chemistry? We talked for fifteen minutes with you and Greg watching us as raptly as a *Hamilton* audience.

Besides, doesn't he have a girlfriend already? I remember he brought a blonde to your barbeque last summer."

"You remember him from then, when you were still with that loser boyfriend, Rick? Your couple potential is better than I thought," Syda gushed. "Greg says Tim's not seeing anyone. Call him. You have a perfect excuse, and he may actually be able to help with your investigation."

Late that afternoon Pat called Mark Bellows instead of Deputy Sheriff Tim Lindsey.

"You have a follow-up report so soon?" Mark Bellows asked. "You haven't even given me enough time to ask you out, yet."

His opening lines flustered her.

"Well, um, I thought you should know as soon as possible, um, so you can work on Joe Wentner's defense."

"Don't get me wrong, I'm not complaining. Do you want to come by my office or shall I come by yours?"

Pat looked around her crowded guest-room-cum-office and quickly answered, "Your office."

"Can you get here by 8:00 tomorrow morning?"

"I can."

"Great. I'll see you then."

The phone call ended, Pat noted, with another tease about a date, but no offer of one. Between that lack of commitment and her dissatisfaction with what she and Syda had been able to discover earlier in the day, she didn't sleep well.

Her puffy eyes revealed how much twisting and turning she endured the night before, so Pat spent more time on her makeup than she usually did. She combed and fluffed her hair with care—*at least my hair is cooperating*—and dressed in lavender, not her favorite color, but not one that would play up her marred eyes. She was ready to see Mark Bellows, but not happy about their meeting on several levels.

She arrived at his office promptly at 8:00, but the office receptionist informed her that he wasn't in yet and told her to take a seat in the lobby. A couple of minutes later, he burst through the entry door using his shoulder to push it open. His hands held two cups of Starbuck's coffee, and one of them also dangled a bag from the same store.

"Sorry I'm late. I got here early and then realized we'd need breakfast. Lead the way; you know where my office is," he motioned her down the hall. "You'll have to open the door," he said when they reached his office.

"I didn't know how you like your coffee, so I got one black and one with cream. Sugar packets are in the bag."

"I'm a with-cream."

"Good. I like mine black, but I'm so gallant, I was willing to sacrifice for you if that's how you like your coffee. I got us chocolate croissants. I figured everyone likes chocolate and everyone likes croissants, unless they're some sort of weird gluten-free type. I was worried about you for a minute and then I remembered you liked your birthday cake, which had both gluten and chocolate in it."

"You're observant. You'd make a good detective," Pat giggled.

"That's your job. What do you have for me?" He handed her the coffee marked "cream," put his coffee on his desk, and added the pastry bag, which he ripped open to display its contents.

"More tantalizing but useless information about Suzanne Cummings, I'm afraid."

"Tell me what you have and let me decide if it's useless, okay?"

"Fair enough. I got Lillian's records of classes Garryn Monteith taught at the Glass House going back eight years. Suzanne Cummings was at every one."

"Wow." He gulped a sip of coffee. "Can you spell stalker in capital letters?"

"I also found other classes he taught in the past, called as many venues as I could find contact information for, and asked the owners to check their class records looking for Suzanne Cummings's name. There were quite a few who found her in their class lists. Then I called female students and asked if they remembered her from the class.

"Most didn't, but among those who did, I asked them why, and also if Garryn Monteith offered them any more attention than he did to other class members."

"And?"

"And I got hung up on a few times, and I had several women say they enjoyed an innocent flirtation with him, and...and I had a couple who said their relationship with him went beyond the innocent.

"Among the women who flirted or more, they all had something happen to them that might have constituted Suzanne Cummings harassing them. One even received a signed threatening letter from her."

"Can we get the letter?"

"No. She got rid of it."

Mark looked crestfallen and took out his vexation with a large bite of croissant.

"What about the others? Anything that they kept?"

"That's the problem. Suzanne Cummings made comments to them that were chilling, implying she had been following them or researching them, but, just like I know she was responsible for my windshield but can't prove it, none of the comments she made were a proof of action. All the women suspected or even knew she was responsible for broken art work, flattened tires, or a broken windshield, but none of them witnessed her doing anything."

Mark had finished his croissant and had to settle for chewing on his lip.

"If I could somehow lay a proper foundation and Judge Blaine happened to be feeling liberal, she might consider letting me bring in attendance records and then a string of women to establish a preponderance of circumstantial evidence. But," he shook his head, "but if I were prosecuting, I'd object and likely win my motion. My foundation would have to be a lot stronger than anything we have now."

"I don't know how you build a defense exactly, and I don't know if you share any information with the authorities. Does letting them know the line of questioning you plan to pursue give too much away?"

"Not necessarily. And when we get to discovery, theoretically things need to be shared anyway."

"I was wondering if what I discovered about Suzanne Cummings's stalking might be good for the Sheriff's Department to know right now. Or not."

Mark pondered for a moment. "Since I don't see how I'm going to get her behavior in front of the jury and establish a point for reasonable doubt without help, I don't see how it could hurt."

Pat smiled. "Good. I have a connection with a couple of deputy sheriffs, including the one who interviewed me about Garryn Monteith's murder. If I have your blessing, I'll let them know what I discovered."

"Go for it."

Mark suddenly flipped his watch up so he could read it. "Ahh. We had to get together at 8:00 because I have an early court appearance. I've got to go right now. Sorry. Bye."

He scooped up his briefcase and left her sitting in his office to finish her coffee and croissant alone. Again, no mention of a date. She wished he wasn't such a busy man.

※※※※※※※※※※※

Pat could have called Greg, but she fingered the card Deputy Sheriff Tim Lindsey had given her instead. He was the one who had interviewed her initially and he had told her to call if she had anything to add to what she told him. It seemed she might. She dialed his number, telling herself calling him was like calling Greg anyway, since he and Greg were still partnering until the end of the week.

"Lindsey," was how he answered.

"Hello, Deputy Sheriff, it's Pat Pirard," she said in a formal voice.

"I thought we had agreed you were Pat, which would make me Tim. What can I do for you?"

"I have some information that I think your department should know about the Garryn Monteith murder investigation. Has it been turned over to someone in particular or can you help me?"

He cleared his throat. "I can help you. I think we should talk in person. Where are you; can I come by now?"

"I'm at home, I have an office here. You can stop by this afternoon." Pat gave him her address.

"I'll be there around 2:00."

Dot at the door, not barking, but being alert with her tail tucked between her legs in an unsure stance, was Pat's first indication that Deputy Sheriff Tim Lindsey was prompt.

Dot still didn't bark when he knocked on the door.

Pat had stowed her lavender outfit and changed into yoga pants and a yellow plaid flannel shirt, comfort clothing, and had taken what she intended to be a mini nap to make up for her sleepless night, but she had been so comfortable that she slept longer than she planned. Her cheeks were still flushed from sleep when she opened the door to Officer Lindsey.

"You're alone? I thought Greg would be with you."

"Not today. He had to testify at court so I'm working solo."

"Come on in. My office is pretty full; it doubles as a guest room. We can sit out here," she pointed to her sofa and quickly moved the throw she'd used for warmth during her nap.

"Fine."

"I can make coffee if you'd like some. You can drink coffee on duty, right?"

"Absolutely, but only if you're having some. We're not allowed to drink alone." His grin was wicked and his blue eyes twinkled. She knew immediately his answer was a prank response.

His wit was so disarming that Pat giggled.

As Pat headed toward the kitchen, Dot took up mistress guard duty next to the sofa where he sat.

"You know I'm working for Mark Bellows, Joe Wentner's attorney, don't you?" Pat used the pass-through to call her question into the living room where Tim and Dot were sizing up one another.

"I do," he called back.

By the time Pat brought the tray of coffee and fixings into the living room, Dot had her head on Tim's knee and was enjoying a head scratch.

"I've discovered some suspicious evidence about a woman in the class at the Glass House that may point to her being Garryn Monteith's real killer," Pat began. "The problem is the evidence is circumstantial—not hearsay—but not something I can prove is true. Mark and I are hoping the Sheriff's Department might be able to firm it up so he can use it in court."

"So you want to tell me about it, have me look into it, and see if it helps Bellows defend the man the DA has charged with murder? Is that about it?"

"That's it exactly, although when you say it," Pat grimaced, "it comes out like an infringement of the way things work, doesn't it? It would be in the interest of justice, though," she added quickly.

He chuckled, "I won't make any promises, but I always want the right person to be charged."

Pat poured coffee for them, spread out her paperwork, and went over the same information she had given Mark Bellows earlier in the day. Officer Lindsey focused closely on what she told him, nodding in what she thought were all the right places, and frowning as often as she did.

"I'll make some follow-up calls, but it seems like you did a pretty thorough job. For a woman who's only been a detective for a week, I'm impressed with what you've accomplished. The one advantage I could have is that with an official inquiry, I won't get hang-ups. That might shake out some more concrete evidence.

"Do you like Frank Sinatra?" he asked abruptly and without a segue.

"What? I guess so. Why?"

"There's a tribute to his music at the Kuumba on Saturday night, and I wondered if you'd like to go with me to hear it."

"Uhh."

"Don't worry. It wouldn't be okay for me to ask you if you were a suspect in the case, but since you're not, there's no conflict of interest."

"You're sure?"

"Pretty much," he said and smiled disarmingly.

Saturday night. That was a date night and she had been hoping Mark would ask her out. But he hadn't, and Deputy Sheriff Tim Lindsey had. And Tim Lindsey was cute...and charming...and funny...and she could wear comfortable clothes around him...and she didn't have to worry that her office wasn't impressive enough...and Dot had clearly given him her Dot Seal of Approval... "I'd like that."

"Great. Just one thing: let's not tell Greg or Syda about this. If it turns out we hate spending time together, they don't need to know we did. And if it turns out we do like spending time together, they really," he emphasized the word, "don't need to know that, at least not until after our tenth date."

No drawn-out lead-ups for him, no mixed messages. Pat added that and his strategy about Syda and Greg to Tim's other attractive qualities.

※※※※※※※※※※※

Pat's phone rang mid-morning the next day. It was Mark Bellows.

He didn't say hello, but launched right into his dialog.

"Hey Pat, I have a conference and dinner with the governor and a bunch of attorneys in San Francisco tomorrow. Would you like to come with me? You'd be on your own tomorrow afternoon, but you could join us for dinner and we could stay overnight and play in the City on Sunday."

Pat's heart rate sped up. *He's finally asking.* Her thrill only lasted for a few seconds.

"Tomorrow is Saturday."

"Last time I checked it was."

"Mark, I wish you'd asked sooner. I already have plans for tomorrow night."

"Well, break them."

Pat had accepted an offer for her senior ball from a guy friend only to have the star football player ask her to go with him a few days before prom night. She had hesitated for several minutes before she told him she already had a date. He suggested the same thing Mark had. She hadn't accepted the late offer then, and she wasn't about to now, even though she badly wanted to both times.

She'd had a great time with her friend, but when she saw the big man on campus at the prom with another girl, it stung. Though her decision hurt, even as a girl she knew she made the right one. As a woman with a fully formed sense of self-worth and principles, she had no hesitation making the same decision now.

"I'm sorry, Mark. I don't behave like that."

"Well, another time, then," he said with a shrug in his voice, and hung up.

The star football player never asked her out again. She wondered if Mark Bellows, the man who made her heart flutter, would.

Pat's ringing phone woke her up on Monday morning. She was ready to complain to her tormentor that 6:30 was too early for someone to call unless they were bleeding and needed her help, but when she glanced at the time on her cell phone as she answered it, she noted that it was 8:45. She panicked for a second before she remembered she was no longer the law librarian, obliged to be at work at 8:30, and realized that she hadn't overslept. In the next instant she saw that her caller was Mark Bellows.

She ran her tongue over her teeth in an attempt to freshen them before she remembered—with a great sense of relief—that he couldn't see her. As she pulled herself upright and pounded her pillow behind into a backrest, she debated how she should greet him after the Saturday fiasco.

Friendly, she decided. She smiled as she spoke to make it convincing. "Good morning, Mark."

"Good morning, Pat." His good morning sounded more formal than sociable. "Could you put together an invoice for the hours you've worked and bring it by my office this afternoon?"

"Of course," she stammered, "if you want me to."

"Great. I'll expect you around 1:00, then."

Pat was dressed in her yellow skirt and high heels and had a green cropped jacket on over a silky cream blouse when she arrived at Mark Bellows's office. Her work log and invoice were in her leopard-print briefcase. If she was going to get fired for the second time in a little over two weeks, she was braced for it.

She was full of righteous indignation as she parked her car in the law office parking lot. It seemed he was willing to overlook how much information she had discovered in a short time. It seemed he was about to fire her, but not for performance. He was going to fire her because she hadn't accepted his last-minute offer of a date and a potential night together—which was something she wouldn't have agreed to on a first date anyway, she reminded herself. If that was what Mark Bellows was about, well then, so be it. He wasn't worth her time.

She stepped into his law office lobby with her head held high, her heels clicking smartly, and her face set into a look of professional detachment.

"Pat Pirard to see Mr. Bellows," she informed the receptionist in a chilly voice.

Her certitude dissolved when he came down the hall toward her smiling like he was genuinely glad to see her.

"Hi, Pat. Come on down to my office."

He directed her to the seat in front of his desk and took up his position facing her from behind his desk. They'd occupied the same places during their last meeting, but this time Pat felt he was using his desk as a shield to keep his distance.

He held out a cup of Starbucks coffee to her. "With cream," he said.

"Thank you." She worked hard to maintain a sense of disinterest. "I have my record of time spent and my invoice like you requested."

She dropped the documents on his desk and watched them closely to avoid making eye contact with him as she used her fingertips to push them in his direction.

"Pat, I can tell you're upset. I'm sorry. This has nothing to do with me being dissatisfied with your work. It's just that Joe…I shouldn't say more because of attorney-client privilege and all that."

"If you tell me something before you dismiss me, aren't I a part of that privilege?"

"Nice try, but, no." He took a few long draws of coffee and said nothing. She wondered if he had ended the conversation and his silence was her cue to leave.

Finally, he cleared his throat. "We might discuss someone I'm representing without naming names, though, now that you don't work for me. Naturally, I would expect our conversation to go no further, especially not to your Sheriff's Department connections."

Pat drew her fingers across her lips in a mime of zipping them.

"I hope I don't make a slipup and say something to them that might help with an unnamed person's case. Anything I say would just be my opinion, though, since I don't work for you anymore, but you do know that I'm a highly opinionated woman." Pat smiled guilelessly. "Or perhaps you don't, since we haven't seen each other except at work."

"About that," he screwed his face into a contrite expression, "I missed you this weekend. Perhaps we can do something about our neglected opportunity as soon as things settle down with Joe's case, I mean with the unnamed case I'm working on." Mark smiled merrily.

The smile Pat returned was more complex than the one she had given him previously.

"I suppose, if you have everything you need, I should be going. Thank you for the work; when should I expect payment?"

"I don't do billing, but I think within a week. After you do get paid, would you consider being on a retainer here? We have a good working relationship, and I'm sure my associates would be interested in your services, too."

"I'd like to think about that."

His fingers raised off his desk like her response startled him. "Uhh, if you need to."

*Sure of himself.*

"In the meantime," he continued, "you haven't finished your coffee and I haven't told you about a frustrating case I'm working on, not as employer to employee, but as a friend to a friend."

Pat crossed her legs and leaned forward as she took a sip of her coffee. "Is it anything I can help you with? As a friend."

He shrugged. "Hard to say. I'm in a conundrum with this case. I have to prepare a defense for my client in a murder trial. I have three possible defenses I could use, but my client is making preparing them difficult. My client professes he didn't know about a long-term arrangement his wife had with another man because no such arrangement existed. His wife also insists there was no such arrangement. He absolutely refuses to let me or anyone who works for me do more than take him and his wife at their word.

"If I was sure the DA didn't have any reliable firsthand witnesses to testify she was cheating, I would put both of them on the stand to say he had no motive for murder because nothing was going on between his wife and the murder victim. Defense number one.

"If someone not in my employ did happen to discover his wife had a long-term arrangement and he knew about it, I'd have to convince him to let me take a different approach. In that case, I'd have his wife take the stand, confess, and say she told him about what she was doing years ago. I could argue, if he knew about her actions and did nothing about them over a period of years, why would he act on old news now? That sort of question might lead a juror to have reasonable doubt about my client's guilt. I would also try to direct the jury to consider someone else who might have a motive for murdering the victim. Defense number two.

"I wish I knew if there were any reliable witnesses out there who would testify that they had firsthand knowledge that the wife was having an affair and that my client did know about it. That would mean both my client and his wife were lying to me—which does happen more often than you would think—but at least it would let me know where to spend my defense efforts."

"How interesting. I understand your problem," Pat said.

"I thought you would."

"What happens if it turns out she was involved and he just found out about it?" Pat asked.

"Then he's screwed and probably guilty," Mark chuckled. "Defense number three will be aimed at trying to make sure he doesn't die in jail."

Pat put her empty coffee cup on Mark's desk. "Well, I better be going. I have a busy day in front of me. Thank you for the coffee."

Pat smiled all the way back to her car. She wasn't really fired, just on a technical Joe-driven hiatus. She wasn't told not to keep poking, quite the opposite. And Mark still seemed interested in her outside of work.

That last realization caused her to cease smiling and bite her lip. After Saturday night, her life might be getting rather complicated. Being around Mark still made her heart beat faster, but the unexpectedly tender kiss Tim had given her as he dropped her off after their Frank Sinatra retrospective had left her tingling from her lips to her toes.

"Work," she said to herself as she slipped into her car. "Work, and don't think about either of those two men."

Pat could redouble her efforts to investigate Suzanne Cummings, looking for instances where her threats were directed at people rather than objects—for Mark's second defense; but Tim was following up on that. She needed a different line of research to pursue until he had a chance to conduct his own investigation.

She started with a quick call to Kandi Crusher for a follow-up question. Either Kandi wasn't screening or she recognized Pat's number, because she answered her phone immediately.

"Hi, Kandi, it's Pat Pirard."

"I know."

I have a question for you."

"Shoot."

"Was it common knowledge in the Glass House classes that Lillian and Garryn were involved?"

"Hard to say. To me it was obvious."

"Why was that?"

"Because of the way Garryn fawned over her and let her play queen to his king in his back-to-work processions. You must have noticed that he led his class—his court— back to the studio with Lillian on his arm after breakfast and lunch."

"I did notice that, and thought like you did, that he enjoyed feigning royalty."

"It's good he's dead. If he heard you suggest he wasn't real royalty, unless you were going to say he was a lesser god, he'd bust a gut."

Pat chuckled. "So, you and I thought we should doff our hats, but what about everyone else? I believe they treated him royally, but did they think Lillian was his queen? You were primed to see things that way because your brother told you Garryn said he and Lillian had a fling whenever he was in town. But did you ever hear any of the students say anything about the two of them? I'm especially interested in knowing if anyone said they saw something between them...besides the procession."

"I'd have to think about that. Right off the top of my head, I'd say no, but I'm not sure."

"What about Joe? Did he ever say anything about them to you? Or did you ever notice him looking at them spitefully?"

"No to both questions. But if you ask me, he was too unaware. You know what I mean? It was like he went out of his way to look somewhere else when the procession rolled by."

"Thanks, Kandi. That's all I needed to know."

"Wait. Don't hang up. Tell me what's happening with Joe."

"He's still charged and still out on bail."

"What's his attorney got you doing now? How is he going to defend Joe? I hope he has some good ideas, because Joe is such a decent guy; it wouldn't be right if he got blamed for ending Garryn Monteith."

"I no longer work for his attorney, so I wouldn't know what his plans are."

"What happened?" Kandi trilled.

"I was let go."

"No foolin'. Then why are you still asking me questions?"

"I'm curious—or maybe nosy—and I have some free time, so I thought I'd ask."

"If you think of anything else, ask again. We curious women have to stick together."

"I will, and Kandi, I agree with you about Joe."

There was no way around it: she'd have to call all the women who had taken Garryn Monteith's classes at the Glass House for a second time. When she tallied up newly added names from the class she'd attended and subtracted duplicates and no-longer-in-service numbers, her new list was long and her task daunting.

She needed to give careful thought to what she wanted to ask this time, because she was determined this was going to be her last ear-numbing phone call exercise.

Pat thought better when she walked, and her mind-reading dog had appeared with her leash in her mouth as soon as Pat got off the phone with Kandi.

"You don't have to give me that sad-eyed, need-to-pee look, Dot. We're going for a walk right now," Pat promised.

Dot dropped the leash at Pat's feet and opened her mouth in a full-on Dalmatian smile.

Pat walked with earbuds in place. Their cord terminated in her pants pocket where they didn't connect to anything. She liked to formulate potential questions and consider how they sounded by asking them out loud, and the unconnected earbuds let her. Passing people assumed she was on her phone, not some deranged woman talking to herself. Sanity was so much easier to fake in the age of the iPhone.

"Did you ever notice Lillian and Garryn flirting?" She shook her head and said, "No. Did you happen to notice Lillian and Garryn touching?" God, no. "What did you think of Lillian Wentner and Garryn Monteith's relationship?" Better. "Did you ever think Lillian Wentner and Garryn Monteith might have had a relationship that was more intimate than a business one?" Getting there. "Did you ever think Lillian Wentner and Garryn Monteith might be more than business associates?" Pat smiled. "There's my opening question."

Follow-up questions were easier to frame; she had them in one try. "Why is that? Did you ever speak to any of your classmates about them?"

Her final question was the one she wanted to ask immediately, but groundwork had to be laid before she could. "What do you think Joe Wentner thought of his wife's and Garryn Monteith's involvement?"

Pat pulled out the earbuds and stuffed them into her pants pocket with her imaginary phone. Sane people could talk to their dog; no one would fault her for that.

"Have you had enough of a walk, Dot? I hope so, because we need to go home now. I have a busy afternoon with lots of phone calls to make."

Pat didn't get a hit in her first twenty-two calls, which covered women in the first class and most of the women in the second class Garryn Monteith taught at the Glass House. She scored with the second-to-last interviewee in the first year of classes.

"Garryn and Lillian? I wondered," Jonsey Meyers said.

"Why is that?"

"You know how people look at one another when they're in love? That's how they looked at one another. Business associates have one way of interacting, and good friends have another way, but lovers? They share special glances."

"Did you ever speak to any of your classmates about them?"

"Not anyone from that class, but I took another class the next year and I saw the same thing going on. I did talk to one woman about it. We sat next to one another in class and were friendly. We both took another class the next year and the same thing was happening. Of course we speculated. There were rumors, too, although I don't know who started them. Word was just out to watch Lillian and Garryn."

"What's the name of the woman you talked to about Lillian and Garryn?"

"Jean something. I can't remember her last name. We didn't take any more classes together after that and we lost touch."

"What do you think Lillian's husband, Joe, thought about their behavior?"

Pat's interviewee let out a snort. "I thought he was either the densest man on the planet or a saint. I couldn't figure out which one he was, though. Oh, I just remembered where I heard the rumor about them. It was from that woman you called about last time. Suzanne."

"Suzanne Cummings?" Pat tried not to sound surprised, but she was.

"Uh-huh. Suzanne Cummings."

Pat had finished as many of the phone calls as she intended to make for the day by 7:30. She was hungry and ready for a late dinner, but by then she had no energy left for cooking. She settled for a bag of prewashed greens dumped in a bowl and topped with a can of precooked chicken. She stared at her uninspiring supper and then reached for the open bottle of Chardonnay in her refrigerator. It needed drinking soon, and a glass or two of wine would finish the bottle and might help make her insipid dinner salad palatable.

Her calls had been productive to a degree. She had tracked down the woman named Jean who Jonsey Meyers referenced, but for her needs, Jean was as much of a bust as Jonsey had been. Jean said that she remembered some elbow poking she and Jonsey had done about a "thing" between Lillian Wentner and Garryn Monteith. She had nothing to add about Joe's awareness of it, though. Joe, it seemed, had only impressed her with his cooking.

Pat did get a few other hits in later classes, but most women were so involved in their work and in admiring the entertaining antics of Garryn Monteith, that they hadn't paid much attention to Lillian Wentner, let alone to her husband, Joe.

Those who did speculate about Lillian and Garryn also remembered there being a rumor about them, a rumor that most said was what started them paying attention to the couple. A few attributed the rumor to Suzanne Cummings, just as Jonsey Meyers had.

Sybil Kreiger, from the first class in the fifth year of Garryn's courses, had more to say, however. Her information might be useful should Mark go for defense number two.

She still had the most recent attendees to call tomorrow; fingers crossed one of them would have something useful to add. And then there was Suzanne Cummings. Somehow, she was going to have to do a follow-up with her.

Pat was finishing her wine when Syda called.

"So, what's the news on your love life?"

Pat turned bright pink. Tim was so clear that they shouldn't say anything about their date to Syda or Greg. Had he? Was it a slip or intentional?

"What love life?" Pat asked, trying to keep her voice as level as she could.

"Has Mark Bellows asked you out yet?"

Pat inhaled deeply and blew out slowly with her cheeks puffed out to muffle the sound. Syda didn't know about her Saturday night with Tim.

"Not yet," she lied. "He did fire me, though."

"He did what?" Syda blasted.

Pat laughed heartily. As she had hoped, she had put Syda off the hunt. She quickly filled her best friend in on the whole story of her dismissal and the backhanded directions Mark had given her about continuing her investigation.

"After I left Mark's office, I spent the rest of the day calling most of the Glass House attendees again pursuing a different angle. I'm beat."

"Why didn't you ask me to help you?" Syda sounded mildly hurt.

"I didn't want to make you do calling again."

"Friends don't keep tantalizing inquiries from friends. I'll forgive you for your oversight if you'll tell me any good stuff that you found out."

Pat told Syda about the infidelity rumors and that it appeared Suzanne Cummings was the source of them. Syda oohed and aahed.

"The worst, or best, bit of information I picked up, depending on what Mark might make of it, came from a woman named Sybil Kreiger," Pat continued. "Sybil had taken a class three and a half years ago and said she was sure Lillian Wentner and Garryn Monteith were, as she said in a classic Boston Brahmin accent, 'carrying on.' She said she talked to Joe about it, too, and that his reaction was 'Oh, that.'"

"So Joe knew?" Syda exclaimed.

"It sure sounds like he did. She said she remembered the details clearly because Joe's reaction wouldn't have been hers if she discovered her husband was fooling around."

"Right on. Greg would be in so much trouble if I ever found out he was cheating."

"There's always the possibility that what Sybil Kreiger told him was new information and that he didn't want to react in front of her. But even if that were true and even if he went ballistic with Lillian in private later, Sybil Kreiger's statement means Joe knew about Lillian and Garryn for a long time—at least three years and many more classes—and did nothing."

"Shuww," Syda whistled. "I never would have thought that Lillian could have such a secret life, but I guess, even though I've known her for a long time, what with both of us artists, I never really knew her. You know what I mean?"

Pat turned pink again. She was keeping a secret from Syda. It didn't rise to what Lillian was concealing, but it made her aware that even best friends could—would—sometimes hide important parts of their lives from one another.

Pat moved on quickly; she didn't want to think about keeping secrets. "Sybil Kreiger said she would be fine with testifying to what she told me if I could get her travel expenses from Boston paid. She sounded calm, clear-headed, and like a reliable witness over the phone. Most importantly, her information was firsthand, not hearsay."

"What do you think it means that Suzanne Cummings was spreading rumors?"

"I'm not sure, yet. I still have calls to make tomorrow.

You might get called on to help after all, too. You may need to talk to Suzanne again because I'm sure she won't speak to me, and I probably wouldn't be civil to her even if she did agree to answer my questions."

"Not again. Last time we tried double teaming her, your car suffered and we weren't too happy with one another for a while."

"Which is why I'm still hoping to spare you. It may all come down to whether or not Tim…Officer Lindsey," Pat stammered, "does some of our work for us. We talked. He agreed to conduct his own investigation of Suzanne Cummings. As long as he's working on finding out more about her, I don't think we should get in his way."

"You talked to Tim again?" Pat could hear the happiness in Syda's voice. "And? Do you want me to arrange dinner for you two with Greg and me? It will be a little more complicated now that vacations are over and they aren't partnering any more, but I'm sure I can still manage."

"Thanks, Syda, but please let it go for now. I have more work to do and a lot of thinking to do about what I'm discovering. I'm too preoccupied to be good company at the moment."

Tim called almost immediately after Pat's call with Syda ended. "How do you feel about fish tacos?" he asked.

"First you ask how I feel about Frank Sinatra, and now you want to know how I feel about fish tacos?" she giggled. "Don't you ever start with, 'How do you feel about me, Pat? Would you like to go out with me?'"

"Way too scary. You might not agree to going out with me, but if I invite you to hear Old Blue Eyes or eat fish tacos...well, everybody likes them. I figure the odds are pretty good you'll say yes."

"Don't be afraid," Pat said coyly. "Ask me straight up how I feel about going out with you."

"Okay. How do you feel about a second date with me? You can't see me because we're on the phone, but I'm cowering waiting for your answer."

"I like Frank Sinatra and fish tacos, too, but that's irrelevant. I like you, Tim. I'd like to go out with you again."

"That's good to hear," he sighed in feigned relief, "because I like you, and I had a great time on Saturday. So, I'll pick you up around 7:00 tomorrow night and we'll head up to the Davenport Road House for Tuesday night fish tacos and music."

Pat had already decided she wouldn't contact Mark with any updates until she received payment for her services, although she badly wanted to hear what he thought of her new discoveries. But after talking to Tim, she didn't give Mark a second thought for the rest of the night.

Eleven to go. Pat steeled herself to call her classmates. At least she wasn't bothering them for a second time, since she and Syda skipped them when they made their Suzanne Cummings calls. And then there was Suzanne Cummings. Pat had written her name in all caps at the top of her list. Seeing Suzanne's name was a repeated cause of anxiety, but with any luck, the call to her could be put off for at least a few more days.

Her questions were friendly—chatty—in the beginning, using their shared trauma of seeing Garryn Monteith die as a conversation starter. It was easy to work asking what they thought about Joe into the discussion—and also asking whether or not they heard rumors about Lillian and Garryn being a couple—without it seeming like either question was the point of her interview.

With a couple of exceptions, the conversations usually ended in the same place: Joe was a sweet man and a great cook, and they were embarrassed to admit it, but there were rumors, not that they believed them.

Pat tiptoed into asking who told them about Lillian and Garryn, expecting to hear the name Suzanne Cummings, but none of them mentioned her. One woman said she heard it from Patty Osgood, another from Regina

Goodman, but all the others named Kandi Crusher as their source.

That tidbit was unsettling. Yes, it was possible Kandi shared the *Same Time Next Year* story with others as she had with her, but something didn't feel right about Kandi spreading rumors. She said she planned to humiliate Garryn Monteith, but a rumor like that damaged Lillian's reputation, too. Why would she do it? Why embarrass Lillian? Most importantly, why hadn't she mentioned that she was sharing tales that might give classmates ideas about Lillian and Garryn? It seemed like Kandi had grander plans than she let on.

Pat didn't have much time to think about Kandi's motive because the last call she made blew every other thought out of her mind.

Roberta Grumm lived in Carmel and hadn't been to any prior Glass House courses. Background information ready, Pat dialed her number.

"Hi, Roberta, it's Pat Pirard from the class at the Wentner…"

"Oh, my God," Roberta pounced, "isn't it awful what happened to Garryn? Our Carmel paper only comes out once a week on Friday, and I was distracted all weekend so I just got to it today, and I saw in the 'Localish News' section that Joe Wentner was arrested for murder last week. Is that true?"

"Yes it is."

"Oh, my God," Roberta's voice rose an octave and the pace of what she was saying, already fast, got faster. "A

Sherriff's deputy from Santa Cruz called a few days ago and asked me if I had ever had any trouble with Suzanne Cummings. I said no—because I hadn't—but he didn't ask me anything about Joe, and I thought since—well, we all were interviewed at the time, weren't we—that he wasn't interested in Joe or in what I know about Joe and Lillian. Well, I don't even know if I know anything about them, but I might, and I'm so glad you called because I wanted to talk to someone, but I didn't know who, and I didn't want to call the Sherriff and get them in trouble when I'm probably wrong anyway."

Roberta finally paused to gulp air. "I'm so glad you called," she whimpered, close to tears.

Listening to Roberta Grumm made Pat feel like she was trying to keep track of a bee buzzing around her head.

"Please, Roberta, calm down. You can tell me what you think you know and we'll work out what you should do together? How does that sound?"

"Oh, my God. It sounds like…that would be wonderful!"

"Good," Pat said. She spoke slowly, reassuringly. "Just relax for a bit—take a deep breath—and when you're ready, start at the beginning and tell me what happened.

Pat listened patiently to huffing sounds on the other end of the phone.

"Okay. I live in Carmel and I love anything by Thomas Kinkaid. Do you know who he is?"

"Yes, I do."

"A lot of people say he's overly sentimental, but I

appreciate his artistry. Well, I was on my way to one of the Thomas Kinkaid galleries, just to look, because I don't have any more wall space."

Pat despaired that Roberta would ever get to the point.

"So this van pulls up as I'm walking by and this man and woman get out of it. They each slammed their door, which got my attention. They were not quite yelling at one another, but clearly they were in the middle of a heated discussion. They kept it up while they went to the back of the van, opened the door, and took out a couple of big boxes. I probably shouldn't have slowed down walking and I should have ignored what they were saying, but you know how it is—and besides, once they got the boxes, we were all walking in the same direction, so I listened in.

"He said he had had it and wasn't going to put up with it anymore. She said he wouldn't have to because she wanted a divorce. Well, I was behind them, and I almost walked into the back of him because he stopped dead in his tracks.

"'You don't mean that,' he said. 'Yes, I do,' she said. 'You always say that before he gets into town,' he said. 'Well this time is going to be different,' she said. 'He always asks me to leave you and I always say no, but this time I'm going to say yes,' she said."

"And you think the people you walked behind were Lillian and Joe Wentner?"

"I had no idea who they were at the time, but when I got to the class, I recognized them. At least I think I did. I just wasn't one hundred percent sure it was them."

Pat was about to take a deep breath herself. If true, what Roberta Grumm said would be devastating for Joe's defense. But Roberta was so doubtful that she could imagine a skilled attorney like Mark Bellows turning her into a wild-eyed unreliable witness and instructing a jury to overlook what she said.

However, Roberta didn't stop there.

"I may not be a hundred percent sure that I recognized them, but I'm sure about recognizing the logo on the boxes they were carrying. It didn't mean anything to me at the time, but when we were in the studio and took our pieces to the kiln alcove for our first firing, there were dozens of boxes stacked against the side wall—you remember that, don't you?—with the same logo on them."

"You're absolutely certain the logo was the same one you saw on the boxes in Carmel?" Pat asked.

"One-hundred-and-ten percent sure."

After her conversation with Roberta Grumm, Pat knew she couldn't wait until she was officially invited back to consult for Mark Bellows's law firm. He needed to know right away that he better start working on defense number three.

"Law offices," the practiced receptionist said in her well-modulated voice. "How may I direct your call?"

"Mark Bellows, please." Pat tried to keep from sounding rattled, but to her ear she didn't seem convincing.

"Mr. Bellows is in court. Would you like to leave a message?"

"Yes, please.

"I'll transfer you."

The sound of Mark stating his name in such a dispassionate manner probably would have soothed her if he had been live, but getting a recorded greeting only flustered her more than she already was.

"It's Pat," she said. "There's a, I think, rock-solid witness who will say she heard Lillian telling Joe she wanted a divorce right before Garryn Monteith hit town. Call me or not; I thought you should know."

Pat kept her phone with her when she took Dot on a longer-than-usual walk in case Mark returned her call. It sat on her desk at the ready while she did a background check of Roberta Grumm, who, it seemed, led a stable and ordinary life.

Roberta, Pat discovered, was married to the same man for thirty-four years. She had three kids who were grown and seemed to have turned out well. She taught art at the high-school level for forty years until she retired a year ago at sixty-two and began to pursue her artistic interests full-time. She might have seemed scattered on the phone, but on paper she was a perfect witness.

Pat noted the time on her cell phone as she checked it to make sure it didn't have a malfunctioning battery. Court never ran later than about four-thirty and it was just past five. Why hadn't Mark returned her call?

By six o'clock she had been suckered into answering a telemarketer call with a local number, thinking Mark might be using an alternative number that she didn't recognize. When her phone rang again at six-thirty, she let it go to the answering function, but sat by, ready to answer it immediately if it was Mark on the line. It wasn't.

She finally gave up waiting and left her phone on her desk. It was time to get ready for the welcome distraction of her date with Tim.

"You're awfully quiet," Tim said as he drove them up the coast toward Davenport. "Is it something I said? Or didn't say?"

"It has nothing to do with you, Tim."

"Is there another man involved?"

He was a good detective. "There is, but not in the way you think."

"You can tell me the truth. We haven't had the 'exclusive' talk yet, so I can't complain if you have multiple interests. And I'm not afraid of some competition. I intend to win your heart, no matter who else is trying to as well."

Pat considered him with fresh eyes. His smattering of freckles made him look boyish, but they were deceiving. He was a man, sure enough of himself to show vulnerability, and brave enough to let her know his intentions even at the risk of rejection. She impulsively leaned toward him and kissed his cheek.

When they had parked at the Davenport Roadhouse, Tim opened Pat's door and offered her his hand to help her out, but he made no attempt to start them walking to the entrance of the restaurant.

"I think your aim was a little off before, because it's hard to kiss someone properly in a moving car. Let's rectify that right now." He took her face in both of his hands, tilted it up, and kissed her full on the mouth. "Much better," he said.

She had to agree.

Pat enjoyed Tim's company on their fish taco date even more than she had on their first date listening to Frank Sinatra wannabes crooning romantically. She giggled and flirted, flicked her hair, and stared into his eyes, but, much as she was enjoying herself, she was never totally present—and he noticed.

"Is it the Monteith case that's distracting you?" Tim asked. "I hope that's all it is. Do you want to know what I found out about Suzanne Cummings?"

Pat knew from talking to Roberta Grumm that someone from the Santa Cruz Sheriff's Department had contacted her. She was pretty sure the officer was Tim. Now he had confirmed it.

"If you can tell me, I do."

"She's a stalker, all right, and not only of Garryn Monteith. She followed and annoyed several women, although I couldn't find any evidence that she ever crossed the line into violence against anything other than inanimate objects like your car.

"She followed Monteith around, too. That's probably why she harassed some of the women she did, because she discovered them with Monteith. If charges got pressed against her for stalking, she might spend a few weeks in jail and be put on probation. But charging her with his murder," Tim shook his head. "I think it would be hard to make a case that she killed him.

"Thanks for doing what you did."

"Hey, it was just part of my job. The fact that I could help out a beautiful woman was just an extra perk."

Pat sat in silence after his compliment.

"I just told you you're beautiful. I expected some sort of reaction." He reached across the table and took her hand. "What's going on?"

Pat licked her lips. She didn't know proper protocol, and Mark hadn't returned her call so she could ask him. Was she obligated to keep her conversation with Roberta Grumm away from the Sheriff's Department to protect her employer's client? Or was she obligated to share what she discovered in the interest of getting to the truth about who murdered Garryn Monteith?

Pat looked into Tim's concerned blue eyes and made her decision: she wanted truth to prevail.

"I've been doing some research on my own and discovered a witness who will say Lillian Wentner was about to leave her husband for Garryn Monteith."

"Holy…"

"I'm not sure if I should be telling you this…and I wanted to. That's what's been in the way all night."

Pat was up and dressed by the time Mark returned her call the next morning. She heard urgency in his tone.

"Pat, I need you in my office right away. You dropped quite a bombshell yesterday. I want you to tell me details so I can convince Joe he has to let you back on the case. If you uncovered a witness, it's just a matter of time until the authorities find your source. He has to start being straight with me so I can mount a viable defense. What you've uncovered may be just the kick in the butt he needs to get realistic."

Mark listened attentively as Pat related her conversation with Roberta Grumm.

"I spoke with Joe this morning and warned him about a potentially damaging witness. He's still spouting defense number one. You said she looks good on paper and sounded believable on the phone, but I've got to impeach her identification. You met her in class. Tell me she wears bottle-bottom thick glasses..."

"She doesn't, Mark."

"...sixty-two, you said..."

"Sixty-three..."

"Does she look like an old hippy? I can ask what she was smoking..."

"She looks like a conservative Carmelite who volunteers her time for useful causes, Mark."

He didn't stop at the sound of his name. If anything, her interruptions made him speak quicker.

173

"She was behind them. That means she didn't get that good a look at them."

"Mark, you didn't let me finish. It's not as much about her recognizing Lillian and Joe as it is about her recognizing the logo on the boxes they were carrying. She saw the same logo on boxes in the studio kiln room. That's what convinced me she knew what she had seen."

Mark tipped his chair back and intertwined his fingers behind his neck.

"In that case, maybe it wasn't them at all. Lillian might use a delivery company to take her pieces to Carmel galleries. I bet with some encouragement, Lillian and Joe will realize that's exactly how they do business."

Mark's words caught Pat off guard. "Did I hear you correctly? Did you just suggest that Joe and Lillian fabricate a delivery person?"

"No. Of course not," he replied nonchalantly. "Attorneys don't encourage their clients to lie. I just wondered, if they think about it, if they'll remember that they do use a delivery company sometimes. I hope it's true because it would make defending Joe so much easier."

"What about Sybil Kreiger? Remember she'll testify that she and Joe talked about Lillian and Garryn Monteith years ago."

"The Sheriff's Department may not find her. Your research has been amazingly thorough. They may not look at everyone you did. She wasn't at a recent Glass House class, and I doubt they'll go back years ago and ask students questions. Besides, she only matters if we go to defense number two. She's looking for a plane ticket out here," he smiled for the first time since their meeting began, "which I'm not going to send her if we go with defense number one.

"I think we better make you an official employee again as soon as possible." His smile was winsome. "We want you committed to the team again. I'll ask Ben Samson to draw up retainer documents today. He does contract law and he can get them ready for your signature by this afternoon. I'm thinking hourly fees the same as we agreed to when you worked for me and a five-hundred-a-month retainer fee. Is that acceptable?"

Pat still thought the sprinkling of gray in his hair made him look attractive and distinguished and that he had the most amazing smile she had ever seen. She was still enthralled by his quick mind. But something had changed in the way she regarded him in the last few minutes. She considered him with her head instead of her heart and he didn't fare as well as he had in the past.

"I don't think so, Mark."

"Seven-fifty then. You drive a hard bargain," he laughed.

"No. I don't think I want to be on retainer here, or anywhere. I want to keep my options open. I'd be happy— delighted—to work for you and your company anytime you ask me to and I accept the request, but I want to consider what I do when I work. It may be that I want to work for an opposing law firm on behalf of their client and not yours. It may be that I want to make my services available to the police, or sheriff, or some other authority. I need the freedom to decide what I want to do.

"I will work on Joe Wentner's case for as long as you need me. I'll explain what I've discovered to Joe and let him know that he better let you work on another defense for him, because the Sheriff's Department knows all about Roberta Grumm. I'll tell him they've probably already interviewed her."

"How did they find her so quickly, I wonder?"

"They didn't find her. I told Deputy Sherriff Tim Lindsey about her last night."

"Fraternizing with the enemy?"

"I don't see it that way. I know how the law works, but I'd rather the truth came out at trials. I'd like to know that the good guys get justice and the bad guys get punished."

"We all would prefer that, but that's a naive hope. Whichever side knows how to use the law wins. That's the reality of it. I understand that and that's why I'm so good at my job. Don't contact Joe. I'll talk to him and let you know if there's more work I need you to do. Take care, Pat."

13

When Pat got home she found a clear glass florist's vase full of yellow daisies in front of her garage door, placed where she was sure to see them. There was a handwritten note attached.

*I know yellow is your favorite color. It's too late for daffodils and too early for chrysanthemums so daisies are the best I could do. Can I see you again on Friday night (notice I'm straight up asking for a date) or am I rushing you?*

Pat put the daisies on her desk and called the Sheriff's Department. "May I speak to Deputy Sheriff Lindsey, please."

"Lindsey."

"Hello, Officer Lindsey. It's Pat Pirard," she made her greeting formal, imagining Greg at the next desk eavesdropping. "I have some additional information about the Wentner case that I would like to discuss with you. Could you stop by my house on Friday at the end of your workday so we can go over it? I know that will be right around dinnertime, so I hope you won't mind working late."

Tim's laughter was quick and good-humored. "You'd make a good code talker. No need, though, I'm here all by myself eating lunch at my desk."

"I didn't know where you'd be or who might be able to hear our conversation. I like the daisies; that was sweet of you. I want to cook us dinner. Do you have any favorites?"

"Whatever you cook will make me happy."

"I do want to work on the case with you, just so you know."

"Yes, ma'am. Friday around 5:30." Tim was suddenly as proper as she had been.

"Did Greg just walk in?"

"Yes, ma'am."

Wimsey bounded onto her lap as she put her phone down.

"You're in charge, my Lord. Dot and I are going to the beach. I need some up-close-and-personal time with some blue sea and waves," she explained to her cat as she stroked his fur. "I've been fired for real this time and I don't know how I feel about it." His purring began immediately and filled the quiet room. "You're such a good listener, Wimsey, I don't know what I'd do without you."

He climbed onto her shoulder, kindly not using claws for traction, and made a leap to the back of his sun-spot chair, ready to assume his house-guarding duties.

Pat changed into yellow high-water pants and a multicolored embroidered top that reminded her of a fiesta and traded her high heels for coral and lime sandals.

"Dot, dog beach?" she called. Her Dalmatian appeared wagging her tail so hard Pat had to make sure she stayed out of its path or risk being lashed. In the garage she grabbed a woven sack filled with doggie beach toys and a well-worn towel for drying a soaked dog and tossed it into her car after Dot. Dot whined softly as Pat backed out, her way of telling Pat to drive faster.

Pat took the beach sack down to the sand, but didn't get out a ball or offer to play tug-a-rope or fetch with Dot. Instead she sat in the sand and watched her pet streak toward the other beach-going dogs, a flash of black and white and wagging tail.

She wished she had brought a pencil and legal pad so she could make notes, but she hadn't. She flattened a patch of sand with her palm and used a finger to draw initials and arrows in the cleared area. She recalled conversations and tried to connect her scribbles to find a killer.

Joe and Lillian said there was nothing going on between her and Garryn Monteith. That wasn't a believable story; too many sources contradicted it. And yet Joe insisted on basing his defense on that narrative.

Sybil Kreiger and Kandi Crusher said they flat-out knew Lillian and Garryn were involved. Roberta Grumm said she heard Lillian and Joe arguing because Lillian told him she was leaving him for her long-standing love and wanted a divorce. Even though she hadn't heard Garryn Monteith's name mentioned, who else could it have been? What Roberta heard backed up what Sybil said about Joe knowing about his wife and Garryn Monteith for some time.

What role did Suzanne Cummings, a confirmed stalker

who attacked possessions or the work of women she saw as interesting to her former lover, play in the mystery? Why was Kandi Crusher spreading rumors about Lillian and Garryn? Both of those questions troubled her.

She had pretty much ruled out Angela Grinardi, Kandi, and even Suzanne as Garryn Monteith's murderer. Had she been too hasty? They all had means and opportunity and varying degrees of motive. Lillian was someone else who had means and opportunity, but if she was about to leave her husband for Garryn Monteith, it didn't make sense that she would kill him.

Joe—it always came back to Joe—had means and opportunity and, if she put all the other facts together, motive. In her sand notes, Joe seemed like the most likely killer in the Monteith saga, but something still didn't sit right with her. Evidence or not, she didn't believe Joe was a killer. There must be a piece or two that she hadn't yet put together to complete the puzzle.

Pat saw Dot running toward her at top speed, her tongue lolling out of the side of her mouth. Sand stuck to her, and the tiny pink part of her otherwise black nose, the defect that kept her from being a show dog, was brighter than normal. Pat had just enough time to grab the dog towel, pull herself into the smallest ball she could manage, and cover herself with it before Dot slid to a stop beside her and shook water, sand, and beach detritus off of her fur. Pat's beach notes were obliterated by dog paws and flying dross.

✳✳✳✳✳✳✳✳✳✳✳

"Syda, best friend, we have to talk to Suzanne Cummings again," Pat said as they sipped coffee together at Syda's house on Friday morning.

"No, please don't ask me to do that," Syda wailed. "Why do you even care about her? You said you are officially and permanently off the Monteith case."

"I know, and I am, but..."

"Are you still thinking about your attorney? If he fired you, we both know that probably means Mark Bellows is history, too."

"I think that's right for a lot of reasons."

"You know I'd die for you, but talking to Suzanne Cummings is asking too much from even your BFF."

"It won't be too difficult. You call her and set something up and I'll show up and ambush her."

"We tried that and all you got out of it was a broken windshield."

"This time you duct tape her to her chair before she notices," Pat snickered, "so she can't escape. After I finish with her, I'll drive home and hide my car in my garage before you release her. Seriously. I have to ask her some questions and I need a way to make sure she answers them. I have no idea how to do it."

Syda rolled her eyes. "So now in addition to fixing your broken love life, I have to figure out how to get Suzanne Cummings in the same room with you. I don't know, could we play some sort of 'you poor dear, here Garryn was about to come back to you and then he was murdered' kind of gambit to get her in our clutches?"

"Maybe. That's a good idea, BFF. Maybe something like that...wait, I've got it," Pat exclaimed. "You still have to be the one to call her. Tell her that some of the class want to make a ghost memorial at the beach. We all have agreed to donate our peonies—throw out a couple of names of students who live within an hour or so away—warn her that I'll be bringing my flower, too, and tell her I want to apologize to her for what I said at Gayle's Bakery. Ham it up about how contrite I am if you have to, and tell her you think she should lead the ceremony because...um...because she was a star pupil and none of the rest of us had that kind of special relationship with Garryn. If you say the right things, she'll bite."

"Great. No pressure. If this works, I demand payback. You have to promise to let me have you and Tim over for dinner within the next two weeks."

"Syda," Pat moaned. "We already met at your house. Remember?"

"You and Tim were sitting at the kitchen table for less than fifteen minutes, and you weren't looking your best. I'm talking dinner, wine, maybe some candlelight...it's non-negotiable."

Pat sighed dramatically to cover her amusement. "All right, if that's what it takes. You're pretty demanding for a BFF."

Pat sat curled up next to Tim on her living room sofa; he had his arm around her shoulders. Dot was on the floor at Tim's feet, pretending to be asleep. It was her position that said: "I like him and approve of him if you do, too, but should you need me to defend you, I'm still ready." Wimsey was in the room, as well—on a facing chair, but nevertheless, present—unusual for him when other people were in the house.

"Are we the picture of domestic bliss or what?" Tim spoke softly. "You probably figured out that I like you a lot, what with being a private investigator and all, and my feelings for you came before I knew you could cook. You are such a talented woman."

"I have many talents you haven't discovered yet," Pat said beguilingly.

Tim reacted to her words with a huge smile. "I like the word 'yet.'" He leaned toward her and kissed her. "You realize we have a deadline now. We have to see each other seven more times in the next two weeks for our ten-date disclosure or non-disclosure plan to be ready by Syda's inducement dinner. Seeing you that much isn't going to be a problem for me. How do you feel about it?"

"I like the idea of spending a lot of time with you. We may even have to throw in a couple of breakfasts down the road if we're going to make it to ten, though."

"I can live with that."

Their next kiss was the best one they'd shared. Yet.

❊❊❊❊❊❊❊❊❊❊

"She agreed!" Syda's voice soared from Pat's phone as she excitedly told her about the conversation she'd had with Suzanne Cummings. "I called her and told her about the ghost memorial. I said I was going to ask Kandi Crusher and Roberta Grumm and Melany Hanson and Lillian Wentner to come, too. She balked at Lillian. She asked if I had a commitment from her and I said I didn't have any commitments from anyone yet because I was starting with her, since she was the one who would be leading the ceremony."

"Great work," Pat congratulated her friend.

"I thought I'd feel guilty lying about inviting the others, but I didn't, not a bit. I guess what I did is like what Greg has said he's done when he's involved in a setup. It's kind of exciting."

"What we're doing is a sting. We talked about how it had to just be the three of us. You did tell Suzanne I'm coming, didn't you?"

"Not immediately. Once she agreed, I told her about you. She almost changed her mind, but I had a well-plotted argument ready to go—I think being a writer has improved my intellectual abilities, which helped me convince her—and she agreed. 'Reluctantly agreed,' she said."

"You said she didn't want Lillian invited. Did you get a sense of why that was?"

"I didn't think to ask about it."

"No problem. I'm curious, though; I'll work it into our

conversation at the beach. When are we doing it, the ghost memorial?"

"Suzanne said she could make it on Tuesday. I said that was fine. So Tuesday at sunset at the Davenport Landing Beach. The access is a little dicey, but the sunsets are gorgeous there and the beach is quiet. It'll make a perfect backdrop for a meaningful ceremony, and if it's hard to get to, that just means it will be harder for Suzanne to escape," Syda chuckled.

※※※※※※※※※※

On Sunday night Pat and Tim shared a picnic dinner— his creation this time—and watched a politically correct film screened by the Santa Cruz Guerilla Drive-In in a field in Ben Lomond.

"Can I invite you to do a repeat Tuesday Taco Night?" Pat asked.

"Things just keep getting better and better between us. Now you're asking me out. I like that."

"I do want to see you, but I have an ulterior motive for where and when."

"Should I be crestfallen?"

"Not at all. I said I want to see you, and I do. It's just that Syda and I are going to do a ghost celebration at the Davenport Landing Beach with Suzanne Cummings on Tuesday evening, and it's so close to the Roadhouse."

"Two birds with one stone. I'm a hurt bird," Tim joked, "but I'll get over it, as long as I see you again. I thought you were finally and officially off the Joe Wentner investigation, though, and hanging out with Suzanne Cummings sounds like you're working. Did your on-and-off attorney turn on again?"

"No. I'm freelancing. I don't like unfinished business. That's another thing you should know about me."

"I don't mind that you don't like loose ends. I think the fact that you're a little OC is kind of endearing," he teased. "I don't like that you're having contact with that Cummings woman, though."

"You said you didn't think she was capable of murder."

"I've been wrong before, only once and it was years ago," he grinned, "but it has happened."

"I don't think you're wrong this time."

"If you're going to be a private investigator, you may come up against some nasty types. I don't want to worry about you. Next weekend I'm taking you shooting," Tim said firmly. "I want you to know how to handle a weapon and how to defend yourself. After I teach you how to be a markswoman, we can talk about you getting a concealed-carry license."

"Okay," Pat replied.

Tim raised his eyebrows. "You're full of surprises. I expected resistance."

"Not from me. We'll go shooting next weekend, but first we need a Taco Tuesday rerun."

Syda hadn't been mistaken about the beach access being tricky. The last five feet of the path required climbing skills. Pat launched her peony toward the sand stem-first so she could use both hands to negotiate the drop. Garryn's attachment system—or the patented design of Leonardo Grinardi—worked well and the flower held together, protruding upward from the sand like a lustrous, as-yet-undiscovered species.

She followed the flower with her mid-heeled, open-toed black sandals—not the best choice for hiking and sand, but something sexy she wanted to wear for dinner later with Tim—and an integral part of the all-black mourning clothing she wore for Garryn Monteith's ghost memorial ceremony.

Color lover that she was, she had added so many shiny bangle bracelets, such large dangly earrings, and such a chunky round-bead silver necklace to her ensemble to mitigate its oppressive darkness, that she clanked as she climbed down toward the beach. Her bare feet complained mightily on the rocky outcroppings and did make her regret her choice of shoes, but once they hit the moist, soft sand, they forgave her errors.

Pat retrieved her shoes and her peony and jingled toward Syda and Suzanne, who were waiting for her. She approached Suzanne with outstretched arms, clutching sandals in one hand and her peony in the other.

"I'm so sorry for your loss," she said as she hugged the startled woman.

"Ahh," Suzanne faulted, "thank you?" Then she said,

"Thank you," for a second time firmly, like she meant it.

"Yes. Garryn meant so much to you. And I think you meant a lot to him, too. You know how he could be, though. Sometimes he forgot how much you meant to him, isn't that right?"

"Yes," Suzanne nodded. "Yes, sometimes he forgot I was once his star pupil."

"Now, I bet you're thinking I'm upset with you about my windshield."

Suzanne stammered, "I don't know what you—"

"Don't be," Pat rushed on without giving her time to deny what she had done. "My insurance covered it, and I was so rude to you that you had every right to be angry with me."

Suzanne forced a weak half-smile. "Well, yes. But I do sometimes overreact, at least that's what my counselor— I'm working with someone about anger management— says."

"You're seeing a counselor?" Pat couldn't believe her luck: Suzanne had just given her the perfect lead into what she wanted to talk about. "But if what you did to my car is an example… Suzanne, I provoked you. Why does your counselor think you overreacted? What else have you done?"

Sunset was approaching and the sky was going to pink and orange, so Pat couldn't be sure of it, but she thought color might have risen in Suzanne's cheeks.

"I've broken a few things," she hung her head and spoke barely above a whisper, "and maybe sent a note or two that I shouldn't have that made it sound like I was going to hurt someone, but I never have." Suzanne raised her head and met Pat's gaze. "I never would."

Syda tried to be helpful. "You mean like you get road rage sometimes? We all do, don't we, and we don't necessarily need counseling."

"No," Suzanne said softly. "It's not like road rage."

"It's because of Garryn, isn't it?" Pat asked gently.

"Yes. Like I did with your car. What you said made me angry, but what really hurt me was that you were right."

"The things you broke, the notes you wrote, were they to women Garryn gave special attention to in other classes?"

Suzanne was silent, but she nodded her head.

Pat made sure she didn't sound confrontational as she directed their dialog. "Joe and Lillian told me you were a regular at classes Garryn taught at their studio. He taught there so often, didn't anyone ever say something to them about you, about you breaking things or writing notes? I'm surprised they let you come back all those times if you were disruptive."

"I never acted out there; there was no need to. Garryn never paid special attention to other women at the Glass House. Not with Lillian there." Suzanne trained pained eyes on Pat. "At least not until you."

"Because they had a relationship?" Pat asked.

"Yes. I knew I couldn't compete with her."

"Then why did you keep going to their classes?" Syda queried.

"I knew one day Garryn would get tired of her. I wanted to be there when he did."

The sun began to dip into the ocean, and the nearby cliffs relinquished their greens and golds in favor of shades of gray and charcoal.

"Shouldn't we get started?" Suzanne asked, clearly indicating she had had enough of their conversation.

It was okay. Pat had the information she needed, even if she hadn't completely made sense of it yet.

They arranged their peonies in a line in front of the setting sun and sat in the sand saying kind words about what Garryn meant to them. Suzanne cried openly and Syda snuffled occasionally.

Pat even wiped a tear from the corner of her eye, not because of Garryn Monteith's death, but because of what a mess his actions had made of so many lives, and because she knew there was more pain to come.

Syda and Pat left after Suzanne when the sun was fully down. "Here, Pat." Syda produced two small objects from her bag. "Greg got these for me. They're clip-on flashlights so we can get up the path to the cliff top hands-free."

"Thank goodness for deputy sheriffs," Pat smiled mischievously as she secured her flashlight on the neckline of her top.

"Should we hurry?" Syda asked as they neared the path. "Aren't you worried she might damage your car again?"

"Not at all. I believe she's over me. Besides, I parked my car a couple of hundred yards up the road where she won't drive by it on her way home," Pat giggled.

It took her more than five minutes to reach her vehicle, remove the clip-on flashlight, climb into her car, and use the flip-down mirror to check her makeup and finger comb her hair to make it tidy after the beach breezes. Even after all that, she dawdled before starting her car. The last thing she wanted was to have Syda spot her making a U-turn on Highway 1 and heading toward the Roadhouse instead of home.

The Roadhouse parking lot was a short walk from the restaurant entrance, not lit, but not oppressively gloomy either, because of passing car headlights. Pat's car was old enough that it didn't have a remote locking feature. She put her key into the door lock and was about to turn it when a hand clamped on her mouth and an arm wrapped around her waist. She was pulled abruptly back toward a dark figure who leaned his lips toward her ear.

"We have to get out of here."

Her heart pounded and her hand began a quick descent into her purse until she realized it was Tim who had her in his grip.

"Sorry if I scared you, but Syda and Greg are inside getting ready to have dinner. You won't believe what I had to do to keep from being seen," he chuckled. "We're going to have to get our fish tacos in town at El Palomar on Pacific. My nondescript Highlander is parked a row behind you and a few cars over. I'll follow you, but you better scoot right now before one of them decides the wait for dinner is too long and they come back out to the parking

191

lot to leave."

14

After the beach memorial, Pat had shelved Suzanne Cummings as a killer. She'd previously ruled out Angela Grinardi as a murderess, too. That left Kandi Crusher and Joe Wentner as her remaining prime suspects.

Kandi's motive for murder seemed weak, and Pat was inclined to believe her when Kandi said she only wanted to embarrass Garryn Monteith. Still, Kandi was named as the source of rumors about Garryn and Lillian, and if she was spreading rumors, was it possible she felt more animosity toward him than Pat thought and was planning to do something else to him other than hold up her completed flower and say, "Me first"?

She had to call Kandi again and find out why she had conducted a whisper campaign. If Kandi had a satisfactory explanation for why she was telling tales, she'd have to rule Kandi out, too, and accept the fact that, much as she liked him and much as her gut told her he was an innocent man, Joe just might be a murderer. Kandi or Joe? It felt like Sophie's Choice to her; she didn't want either of them to be guilty.

Pat put off the call to Kandi for most of the day, but by Wednesday evening the weight of ignoring what she had to do had become too heavy a burden for her to carry.

Steeled, she made her call to Kandi, but she didn't reach her. She was thwarted by the voice of George Crusher, Kandi's husband.

"Yeah, well she's not here. She went up to the City to take care of her mother. Mom had a fall—she missed the last three steps into her basement—lives in San Fran in a hundred-year-old house in the Mission where houses have narrow steps and laundry in the basement—didn't break anything, which is a miracle 'cause she's in her eighties and has osteoporosis—but she's bruised and real sore and pretty upset—I don't blame her, I would be, too, if I did something like that at her age."

Pat wondered how many more details he had to give in his narrative of misfortune and woe.

"So Kandi's up there for a few days. I can tell her you called. What was your name again?"

"Perhaps you could give me Kandi's cell number and I could call her at her mother's."

"Oh, yeah, that would work. Mom's probably making her crazy by now. I bet she'd welcome someone to talk to about anything but near-death experiences," he laughed.

Pat wrote down the number George Crusher gave her. She read it back to him to be sure it was correct; she didn't want to call him again.

She checked the clock; it was only 7:10. She could call.

Kandi answered her phone after two rings. A cacophony of jingles, clinks, and murmurs in the background competed with her voice.

"Kandi, it's Pat Pirard. You said to call if I had more questions."

Kandi's voice boomed, "Yeah, I did. Give me a minute to get to another room."

Pat waited for Kandi to speak again as the background noise faded.

"Hi, Pat. My mom's a bit hard of hearing. We were watching *Wheel of Fortune* with the volume up pretty high."

"Your husband told me about her fall. Is she recovering?"

"She's recovered physically; psychologically she's still shaken up. I'll stay one more day and then I'm heading home. What's up?"

Pat decided to be straightforward. "I've been calling our classmates. Your name came up several times and not necessarily in a good way. Why did so many of them say they heard rumors about Lillian and Garryn from you?"

"Because it's true. I was telling stories about them."

"You were repeating what your brother told you about them? Why, Kandi? I get it that you didn't like Garryn and saying negative things about him must have felt good. Telling students that he was a philanderer imputes his character, but to link him with Lillian demeans her, too. Joe insists he didn't know about his wife and Garryn. If what you were saying was news to him, hearing it might have hurt him badly, especially with an audience around to watch his reaction. Why were you doing that?"

"Crap. I didn't think about the audience part. I like Joe.

195

I don't believe for a minute, though, that he didn't know about what was happening right under his nose. He's a kind man, weak though, I think, to let his wife carry on like she did for so long. If I were in his shoes, I would have left her or at least given her an ultimatum. But I shouldn't judge their marriage—and I never meant to hurt him.

"And Lillian? I didn't care about her. I don't like the way she treated her husband, but at least it was all ending."

"You mean she was finally leaving Joe?"

"No. I told you before, didn't I? Garryn dumped her."

Pat frowned. "Why do you think that? Did someone tell you something?"

"No one told me anything; my knowledge is firsthand. I forgot my purse in the studio after the first day of class. I went back to get it before I drove home. I heard them the minute I opened the studio door. They were in the kiln alcove and all lovey-dovey at first, and Garryn was saying"—Kandi slipped into an imitation of him—"'When are you going to leave that wimp of a husband and come back to New York with me?' Lillian got all giggly and said"—Kandi mimicked again—"'As soon as the class is over.' She said she had even told Joe she wanted a divorce.

"I couldn't see them because of where they were, but they got really quiet. I thought they were probably planting big sloppy kisses all over one another. I grabbed my purse and started to leave when I heard Garryn say, 'What do you mean? No. No you can't come with me.' Then Lillian said, 'But you asked me to. You want me to, don't you?' And Garryn said, 'No, I don't.' Their voices started getting louder and Lillian yelled, 'Then why did you ask me to go with you?' and Garryn yelled back, 'Because you always say no!'

"That did it. They started having a huge fight. Lillian was screaming with rage and Garryn was yelling back. Garryn was awful. Cruel. No surprise. He said he'd been over her for years, but considered his classes at the Glass House as a 'lucrative booty-call.' Can you imagine?"

"Lillian must have been devastated."

"Big time. No more *Same Time Next Year* for him."

"So Garryn was the one who ended their affair?" Pat asked incredulously.

"Absolutely. I could still hear Lillian howling from outside after I slipped out of there, that's how loud their fight had become. Then last thing I heard him yell was that tomorrow was the final day for him, that he was never going to teach another class with her.

"I started spreading rumors about them so when I exposed him as a thief and a rat, the class would already be looking at him sideways. I never thought about how it might make Joe look, and I didn't care how it might make Lillian look. Now I'm kind of sorry I did it."

"Kandi, there's a witness who heard Lillian asking Joe for a divorce. It looks bad for him, like Lillian leaving him gives him a good motive for killing Garryn Monteith. If the affair was over, his motive gets weaker. Are you willing to testify in court to what you just told me?"

"Of course, especially if it helps Joe. There may be someone else who can back up my story, too. The

197

bathroom crier hadn't left the property yet, either. When I came out of the studio, I saw her hovering—hiding is a better description of what she was doing—in the plants by the alcove window. If I could hear Lillian and Garryn from outside, she could have, too. She may even have been able to see them if she peeked in, which is what she seemed to be trying to do. I passed her on my way to my car, but she was so intent on spying, I don't think she even saw me leave. Talk to her."

"That's exactly what I plan to do next. Thanks, Kandi. Give my best to your mother."

Pat ended the call and started to call Syda, thinking she might have to be the one to get through to Suzanne, but she hit cancel before the call started. After last night, Pat decided she should try herself. Amazingly, Suzanne answered.

"Suzanne, it's Pat Pirard."

"I know. My caller ID said it was you."

Pat was unsure what to expect from mood-swinging Suzanne. She'd answered her phone so that boded well, but were they still on cordial terms, or had the bond they established the night before disintegrated? With Suzanne it was impossible to predict.

Pat spoke softly, seeking permission before she continued. "May I ask you a question?"

"Okay."

"Did you witness Lillian and Garryn's breakup?" She held her breath after she asked.

"Maybe."

Too far. Too fast. Too blunt. Pat tried to think of how to rephrase. But before she could, Suzanne picked up her story.

"I knew about it, though," Suzanne said. "I thought you understood."

"What do you mean, Suzanne?"

"Garryn didn't flirt with other women at the Glass House classes," Suzanne spoke hesitantly, "because of Lillian. But the first day, he acted like he was interested in you. He acted like he did at other classes when Lillian wasn't around. I knew what that meant. I knew he had finally gotten bored with Lillian and that my chance was coming."

Suzanne lapsed into what seemed like an interminable silence, and Pat began to wonder if she wasn't going to say anything else. When she spoke again, Suzanne teased out her words.

"Maybe I more than thought they were breaking up. Maybe I did see something, or at least heard something."

Pat waited through another boundless pause, but she was beginning to recognize how Suzanne's process worked. She didn't try to push her to go faster.

Finally, Suzanne began speaking again in a slow, whispery voice, as if she had put herself in a trance so she could not only recall, but see what she described.

"I saw him go back to the studio after people started leaving the first day. I waited for the class people to leave and then I followed him. I wanted to talk to him and let him know I still loved him. Except I didn't get inside.

Before I could, I heard shouting. He and Lillian were having a big row. They were so loud I didn't need to go inside. I could hear every word they were saying through the alcove window. It was open a crack, so that made it easy."

"What did you hear?" Pat asked, mirroring Suzanne's halting and breathy speech.

Suzanne's pace hastened and she sounded gleeful as she continued. "Lillian said she was ready to leave her husband to be with Garryn. But he said he didn't want her. He never wanted her, you see. He just used her for sex. He never loved her; not really, not in the way he loved me."

"What you heard was Garryn ending his relationship with Lillian?" Pat asked. Suzanne spoke in enigmas, and Pat had to be absolutely clear about what Suzanne was saying.

"Yes."

Two witnesses. Pat took a deep breath. She had confirmation of what Kandi had said.

"He never would have loved you, either, you know," Suzanne added, her words delivered in a manner that fell somewhere between bitterness and triumph.

"Of course not. I could never have had the connection with him that you did."

"That's right. His flirting with you didn't mean anything to him. Not really. It was just his way of starting to break up with Lillian. Things go wrong along the path to true love; that's just reality. He may not have realized it that night, but if he'd had more time, if he spent more time with me, he would have made me his star pupil again. I know he would have."

Her heart broke for Suzanne. "Yes, I'm sure you're right. Thank you, Suzanne."

Pat put her phone down slowly. She had heard from two sources that Lillian had a motive for killing Garryn Monteith. Now, she had only two remaining questions: what to do next, and how to get Lillian to admit her guilt.

Pat had several options. She could call Mark Bellows again and tell him that, even though he had truly terminated her this time, she was still snooping and had continued asking questions. She could let him know she had discovered Garryn Monteith ended the affair between Lillian and him. She could sit tight for the time being and let Tim know about her discoveries on Saturday morning when he took her for a shooting lesson. She could even use a back door to the Sheriff's Department and let Greg know what she discovered. He'd be receptive; Syda might already have primed him.

She didn't do any of those things, however. Instead, on Thursday morning she called Lillian and invited her over for coffee and chocolate cake.

"Lillian, how are you holding up?" Pat asked solicitously.

"Okay, I guess. Joe's arraignment is tomorrow so he and his attorney are working hard to get ready. You probably knew that already, since you work for Mark Bellows."

"Worked for Mark Bellows," Pat corrected. "I haven't been employed by him for several days. I'm feeling kind of bad about that and I know this is a difficult time for you, too, so I wanted to invite you to my house tomorrow afternoon. I feel the need for cake, chocolate cake especially, because there's nothing like eating chocolate for commiseration and mood boosting."

"I don't think we can make it..."

"Not you and Joe. Just you."

"I don't know. I want to be with Joe when he's arraigned."

"Arraignment is a procedural event with a judge. It's not like trying to impress a jury with a wife's devoted support. Joe will be fine in Mark's capable hands; you don't need to be there. Come eat chocolate cake with me tomorrow, say at 3:00?"

"Joe's arraignment is at 10:00. You know a lot about court proceedings, don't you? Do you think his arraignment will be over by then?"

"Arraignments, in addition to being boring, are quick. Joe should be out of court well before 3:00."

Lillian brightened. "Then I can be a good wife, even if it's only for the judge's sake, and get some chocolate cake, too. Okay. I'll see you tomorrow. Thank you for the invitation and for your support."

"Oh good. I'm looking forward to seeing you," Pat said in a voice that was silky and without a trace of guile.

The cake Pat planned to serve was left over from last

Friday's dinner with Tim. It was an old family recipe she made to impress him. Now the cake, somewhat protected from severe drying by its thick frosting and a covered container, was a bit stale. *Just the sort of thing to feed a woman as you accuse her of murder*, Pat thought as she brought it out of the refrigerator, cut off the exposed slice ends to freshen it, and made coffee.

She made other arrangements, too. "Dot, we're having company. Time for you to dress up. I want you to wear this cute bandana collar."

Dot gave out a single small woof when the doorbell rang and pranced to the front door ahead of Pat, her ever-wagging tail swinging merrily.

"Lillian," Pat smiled evenly, "come in. How did the arraignment go?" she asked as Lillian passed her in the doorway.

"It was like you said it would be. The judge read the charges against Joe, asked him if he understood them, and asked him how he plead. Joe stared straight at the judge and said 'not guilty' in a firm voice. The judge set the trial date for the 26th and then we all left. Murder in the first degree; what happened seemed so perfunctory for such a momentous charge."

"Indeed," Pat said, nodding sympathetically. "Come with me. We have to have our coffee and cake in the kitchen. My dog, Dot, loves chocolate, but it makes her violently ill. I don't have a dining room, and if I put the cake on the coffee table in the living room, well, she once grabbed an entire chicken off of there and ran with it through her dog door into the backyard. By the time I caught her, she had eaten about half of it, all while running at full speed."

Lillian laughed out loud. "I wish I had seen that."

"Trust me, you don't. She's going to sit at attention between us and beg us for crumbs, but don't feel sorry for her and don't give her anything. I have safe doggy treats for her, so even if she looks like she's suffering. She isn't. It's just an act."

"That could be hard," Lillian said as she patted Dot's head. "Look at those eyes, and her bandana collar looks like a bib, she looks so ready for a snack."

They sat at the kitchen table while Pat served coffee and cake, and as advertised, Dot took up her position sitting upright between them. Pat watched Lillian carefully. As soon as she put a forkful of cake in her mouth, Pat asked, "How far are you willing to let this all go before you confess to killing Garryn Monteith?"

Pat expected a reaction from Lillian, but not the casual one she got.

"That may be up to Mark; I guess he told you his idea. You did such good work for him finding that crazy stalker woman and those other two women in the class with potential motives, I'd like to see him create a doubt defense because of them. He doesn't think he can make it work, though. Mark says he'll probably pull the 'we both had motives to kill Garryn' idea out of his bag of tricks, but it seems risky to me. I don't want anyone to think I killed Garryn, even if it's just a ploy. What do you think of that defense?"

Pat gulped coffee. The cake was dry and she needed time to think. "That's one defense he didn't mention to me. The three women you mentioned: they've been ruled out as viable suspects. That's why he doesn't think he can use them."

"Oh, I know, but Mark said he just had to make them sound like possibilities to cause confusion and doubt in the jurors' minds. He didn't have to prove they were guilty of anything. I'd really like to see him try using them."

Pat relished what she planned to ask next. "Did Mark tell you all the rest of what I discovered?"

"What do you mean?"

"I found witnesses who will testify that you and Garryn have had a long-standing occasional affair and that Joe knew about it."

Once again, Lillian remained unruffled. "It's true, Pat. I'm not necessarily proud of myself," she shrugged. "Joe and I had a sort of open marriage. He didn't mind. Most people, most jurors, probably wouldn't understand how our marriage worked, though, and might become biased against us because of it, which is why Mark didn't want to tell them about us. But since there are witnesses, I guess he'll have to."

"There's also a witness who overheard you and Joe arguing, and you saying you were going to divorce him."

Lillian's response wasn't as quick as it had been to Pat's earlier remarks, but when it came it was dismissive.

"Oh, that. Every time we argue about anything, one or

the other of us threatens divorce. We've been married for eighteen years, so obviously saying 'I want a divorce' is no more than an idle threat."

*Doesn't this woman have any buttons?* Pat wondered. *I'm pushing everything I can think of and nothing's happening.*

Dot started to her feet. "Sit, Dot," Pat said as she gave her a treat. "There is one other bit of information I discovered recently."

"What's that?"

"Garryn was ending his relationship with you, wasn't he?"

Lillian dropped her fork. "Oh, how clumsy of me," she exclaimed.

*Finally*, Pat thought. *A reaction.*

"What gave you that idea? What does Mark say about that theory?"

"Since this is information I discovered after my employment ended, I haven't told him about it yet or given him my source."

"But you've...probably mentioned your idea to other people...already—like Syda. I know you two are friends. You probably talk about all sorts of things."

"We do. Right now she's interested in my love life," Pat giggled, "but you're the first one I've told about Garryn calling off your affair and saying he wouldn't be teaching classes at your studio any longer. I thought you should hear it from me even before I told Mark."

Lillian smiled weakly and said nothing.

Pat wanted to scream. She had planned her questions so carefully. Each one should have shaken Lillian—Pat had excitedly imagined Lillian acknowledging Garryn's cruelty as he ended their relationship and delivering a sobbing confession about how she killed him in a sudden fit of passion. But other than a dropped fork and a bit of hesitation, she had obfuscated every answer.

Their conversation concluded with Lillian successfully evading any incriminating answers to Pat's questions or even acknowledging that Pat was right about her relationship with Garryn ending. She remained cool and her responses were so artless that, even to Pat, she sounded like an innocent woman. But as Pat and Dot walked her toward the front door, Lillian finally made a mistake.

"You really haven't told anyone that Garryn broke it off with me?" she asked.

Pat could feel the muscles in her stomach contract. "I haven't had time to yet, and I have a meeting in about twenty minutes that I need to leave for right away," Pat lied artfully. "Mark will probably have left his office by the time it ends. I don't have a private phone number for him, so unless you do, I won't have a chance to speak with him until Monday morning.

"I also want to tell the authorities what I discovered, and I will, but I have this weird code: I think Mark should know first, and with Joe's trial date weeks away, I don't have to rush my information to the Sheriff's Department."

As she started to leave, Lillian grabbed Pat and pulled her in for a hug.

Pat did a fist pump after she closed her front door behind Lillian. It was a small misstep, but Lillian had essentially admitted Garryn had broken off their relationship, and Pat had it on tape. It wasn't enough to convict Lillian, but coupled with Kandi's and Suzanne's testimony, it would be highly damaging.

"Sit, Dot." Pat unfastened the special blue bandana she had made for Dot and put on her everyday red collar. Pat praised her dog. "You were such a good girl sitting right where I wanted you to so the recorder under your bandana picked up everything Lillian said."

Dot displayed a huge Dalmatian smile. If asked, Pat would have sworn Dot understood her completely and had enjoyed doing her part to snare a criminal.

Pat had no code, weird or otherwise. She had no meeting scheduled that would prohibit her from calling Mark Bellows immediately. What she did have was a potentially hours-long wait to hear from Tim. A high-ranking government official was making a brief stop in Santa Cruz, and every law enforcement officer was on duty to protect her, Tim included. He had promised to call when he got a break.

Pat was even keener to talk to him than she usually was because she wanted to tell him all her Lillian news. She glowered at her silent phone as hours passed. Once she aimed spread fingertips at it like a conjuring magician and shouted at it, "Ring. Ring, will you?" No matter what she tried, not matter how hard she willed it to ring, it refused.

By the time Tim's call finally came at a little before 8:00, she had replayed the Lillian tape several times and had mastered speeding through it to the part she considered the good stuff.

"Tim, it's so good to hear the sound of your voice."

"Me, too," his voice sounded husky, sexy.

"Not that that's not what I mean, but that's not what I mean," she said, speeding past how he sounded to her and how it made her feel to get to the business part of their call.

"Lillian Wentner has become my prime suspect. Both Suzanne Cummings—I know, she won't hold up well on the stand—and Kandi Crusher—who will—heard Garryn Monteith break it off with Lillian after the first day of class. Both said he was nasty to her and that she didn't take his rejection well.

"I invited her over for coffee today and recorded her while I questioned her. She was cool until I got to the part, well, here. Listen. We talked more, but this is the important part," Pat said as she brought the tape to her phone mic.

*"Since this is information I discovered after my employment ended, I haven't told him about it yet or given him my source."*

*"But you've...probably mentioned it to other people...already—like Syda. I know you two are friends. You probably talk about all sorts of things."*

*"We do. Right now she's interested in my love life, but you're the first one I've told about Garryn calling off your*

*affair and saying he wouldn't be teaching classes at your studio any longer. I thought you should hear it from me even before I told Mark."*

*"You really haven't told anyone that Garryn broke it off with me?"*

"Did you hear that? She admitted Garryn broke it off with her. Two witnesses and her own words. She has motive!"

Tim's response wasn't what she expected. "I get off in two, two-and-a-half hours. I want to spend the night with you."

A smile tickled the sides of her mouth. She replied coquettishly, "Isn't the first-night-together invitation usually the woman's prerogative?"

"That's not what I had in mind. Not that I'd mind..."

"You wouldn't mind? How romantic of you," she teased.

"Pat, I heard something on that tape that I think you overlooked. Lillian Wentner wanted to make darn sure you hadn't told anyone about her. I'm worried about you. I'm worried about your safety."

"Don't be. I know how to take care of myself."

"I'm sure you do..."

"Besides, she killed Garryn because she felt betrayed and used. Her actions were passionate and impulsive. She was so composed and in control when I questioned her; she wouldn't do something rash again, not because of what I said to her."

"If she picked up the nearest weapon she could find and smashed Monteith over the head, that would have been murder in the heat of the moment. She didn't do that. She may not have thought long and hard about it, but if she killed him, she planned what she did. Now you've given her a reason to think you're a threat to her, one that she can eliminate by eliminating you. The first murder is hard; after that it gets easier."

"That's a tired old cliché…"

"Just because it is, doesn't make it any less true."

Pat took a deep breath. The conversation they were having wasn't the one she wanted. "I'll see you tomorrow at 9:00 for my shooting lesson…if you still want to see me tomorrow. But for tonight, we both better sleep in our own beds. Goodnight, Tim."

※※※※※※※※※※

Between having heated words with Tim, thinking about his concerns, dismissing them, rethinking them, checking that all her doors and windows and even the dog door were locked, and checking her nightstand drawer repeatedly, Pat hadn't slept well.

She had finally fallen asleep at about 5:10, at least that was the last time she checked her bedside clock. But at 6:00, a Dot-in-extremis who couldn't open her dog door stood by Pat's bed whimpering and holding her leash in her mouth, begging to go out. Dot couldn't be ignored; Pat had to get up, even though she felt about as refreshed as if she had just disembarked from a cross-country flight.

"Okay, Dot. I understand. We'll do a quick walk so you can take care of necessities. I'm sorry about your door, but Tim discombobulated me—and not in a good way. I'll explain while we walk."

Pat didn't take time to shower, get dressed, or put on makeup. All she managed was to run a brush though her hair.

"I don't think the neighbors want to see me in my robe, do they, Dot?" She went more formal: she threw a dress-up black wool jacket on over her plaid cotton pajamas.

"Let's go, girl. No comments about how I look. At this hour on a Saturday morning it's not like we're going to see anyone we know."

Dot squatted in Pat's miniscule front yard as soon as they were out the door, and then did more. "Good girl," Pat said as she dropped her doggie policing kit on the walkway. "I'll clean up when we come home, but now I don't have to carry your rake and bag with me while we walk. We'll go to the end of the block, though, as a reward for you being such a good dog after I trapped you inside all last night."

Pat talked to Dot nonstop as they strolled along, gesticulating wildly with her newly freed hand. She explained her Lillian theories and Tim's reactions to them. Between her outfit and her actions, she might have been mistaken for a homeless woman walking her sidekick dog.

They'd only passed three houses when Pat recognized an out-of-place blue Highlander parked on the other side of the street. She tugged Dot's leash and pulled her across the road. Dot sniffed the air as they approached the SUV and her tail began wagging. By the time they reached the vehicle, Dot was pulling her mistress.

Tim was asleep inside his Highlander, semi-upright, mouth open, scruffy more-than-five-o'clock shadow breaking through along his beard line: a perfect match for Pat's disordered look.

Pat rapped on his driver's side window. Tim startled awake and zipped it down.

"Officer, I'd like to report a disheveled man sleeping in his car in a residential neighborhood," she laughed.

He stretched and twisted his head to loosen the stiffness in his neck. "To be fair, I didn't sleep much," he replied.

"You were keeping watch over me, weren't you?"

"I know you can take care of yourself. I was just..."

Pat leaned in through the open window and kissed him.

After pancakes and a shower, Pat put on makeup and dressed in turned-up jeans and her pink tee-shirt—good for shooting, she thought. She added a rainbow-colored scarf but skipped any jewelry because she knew it would get in the way. She refused to wear sensible shoes, however; she loved her yellow stilettos too much to skip them. While Tim showered, she filled her leopard-print briefcase with the day's necessities so she could skip a purse.

"I couldn't shave—no razor—and I don't have a change of clothes here, so I'm clean, but my clothes aren't," he apologized as he toweled his hair.

Pat shrugged. "Maybe we should change that, although I like the day's growth on your chin."

They arrived at the shooting range a little after 9:00. Tim took his service revolver, a small derringer, and a rifle out of his vehicle. Pat slung her briefcase over her shoulder.

"I'm going to teach you how to use all of these weapons," Tim explained, "just so you're comfortable with them, but we'll work on the derringer the most. It might be a good choice for you to have for protection."

Tim was all business when they reached the firing arcade. "Let's start with the derringer. This is a nickel boron gun," he said as he showed her the weapon. "I think once you get used to shooting it, you'll like it."

"Umm, I don't think so," Pat shook her head. She flipped open the flap on her briefcase and produced her own weapon. "I'm partial to .357 magnums and I like this weapon. It's a Smith & Wesson 27 with a five-inch barrel. It fits nicely in my briefcase or nightstand drawer."

She skillfully loaded bullets into the chamber, took a feet-spread stance, and fired at the target down the range.

"I think when we check," she said, "we'll find all my hits in the center circle. I'm a little out of practice, but shooting is like riding a bicycle: once you master it, you never forget how to do it."

Tim was speechless.

"I've had a concealed-carry license since shortly after I went to work in the Law Library. All sorts of characters come in there and not all of them are lawyers. I thought I should be able to defend the staff and my patrons if need be."

He leaned over her and kissed her softly. "You do realize I'm falling in love with you, don't you?" he asked.

It wasn't the romantic setting she had envisaged to hear those words, but she didn't mind.

※※※※※※※※※※

As she told Lillian she would, Pat called Mark Bellows on Monday morning.

"I know I don't work for you, but I have some new information you need to know if you're going to defend Joe Wentner properly."

"Shoot. What have you got?"

"I need to bring you something; we can't do this over the phone."

"I have court this morning in about an hour. How fast can you get here and how fast can you talk?"

"Not that quickly and not that fast. When do you get out of court?"

"We could meet for a late lunch."

A week ago, she would have been thrilled with his invitation. Situations change.

"I'd prefer to meet in your office. Will you be back there by 3:00?"

"Let's make it 5:30, and we can have an after-work drink while we talk."

"Let's make it 3:00," Pat replied.

"I've been busy," Pat said as she began presenting Mark with her findings.

"I'm going to have to pay you for your time."

"Consider my time as a thank-you gift. I appreciate you taking a chance on me and being the first of, I hope, many attorneys to hire me."

He seemed fidgety, like he was about to say something and decided against it. Finally, Pat began.

"Let's start with Kandi Crusher. She overheard Garryn Monteith breaking up with Lillian Wentner after the first day of class. Suzanne Cummings confirms that; she was also eavesdropping. Both said Garryn was horrible to Lillian. It gives her a motive for murder. I also have a tape of Lillian—I made a copy of it so you can listen to the whole thing—but the pertinent part is Lillian asking me for reassurance that I hadn't told anyone about Garryn breaking it off with her."

"Did Lillian know she was being taped?"

"No, but that doesn't matter in California, does it?"

"Not as long as you were the one making the recording."

"You must feel like you're in an awkward place, Mark. You can defend your client, but your best defense is going to damn his wife."

Mark smiled, "Don't worry about it, Pat. I have a plan. I always have a plan. I'd tell you about it over dinner, but since you don't work for me anymore, our privacy clause doesn't apply. We'll have to wait until after the trial to have dinner together."

Pat smiled demurely, but didn't respond.

"Oh, you should know, I'll be calling you as a witness," he tossed the words out as an afterthought. "Will you agree to testify or do I need to subpoena you?"

"I'll be there."

Pat would have attended Joe Wentner's trial even if she wasn't going to be called to testify. She began watching with jury selection. The answers potential jurors gave to attorney questions, as well as where the attorneys used their peremptory challenges, gave hints about the Prosecution's plan of attack and Mark Bellows's plan to defend against it.

The Prosecution favored professional women; Mark liked blue-collar men. Based on those simple and stereotyped profiles, she thought the Prosecution was looking for women who would not be sympathetic to a cuckolded husband who killed his wife's lover, and Mark Bellows wanted men who would be.

If she was right, Mark won a slight edge in the jury-selection phase of the trial. The final empanelment was five women and seven men.

※※※※※※※※※※

Day two of the trial began with an early-morning call from Syda. "Are you testifying today?" she asked.

"I don't think so. I'm supposed to be ready to, but it

looks like they won't get to me until tomorrow. Today will just be dry testimony: the coroner, the investigating officers, stuff like that."

"The investigation officer?" Syda's voice rose melodiously. "That's Tim. Let's go watch him." Syda made no attempt at hiding her enthusiasm. "Oh, and Greg will be testifying, too, as one of the first officers on the scene."

"I went yesterday and am planning to go every day, Syda."

"Oh goodie. Let's go together today. I can watch my handsome husband and take notes for my book—I think there will be a trial in it somewhere—and you can get a nice long look at Tim. He has such attractive blue eyes, you know."

"I hadn't noticed," Pat replied, glad that they were on the phone and Syda couldn't see her smile as she thought about how Tim's blue eyes had a hint of green in them.

"I want to get a look at your lawyer, too. If he's good-looking enough, I may want you to give him another chance." Syda laughed heartily. "I'll see you in court."

Syda got to court first. She sat next to Greg in the second row behind the Prosecution table and twisted in her seat so she could look over her shoulder. When she saw Pat, she waved and motioned her forward.

Pat walked down the outside aisle and slid down next to Syda. Judge Blaine entered right away, everyone obeyed the call to rise, and the judge hammered the courtroom to order.

The prosecuting attorney was called to address the jury. Pat recognized the assistant district attorney assigned to the trial, but she only had a nodding acquaintance with him. She couldn't remember if Robert Smith went by Bob, Rob, or Robert when he wasn't in a courtroom. She decided he looked like a Bob.

"The evidence against Joe Wentner is overwhelming," the assistant DA stated matter-of-factly when he was asked to present his opening argument. "Joe Wentner premeditated and carried out the murder of Garryn Monteith because he was jealous of the murder victim's relationship with his wife." The assistant DA, a pudgy, middle-aged-workman sort of lawyer, didn't add anything more. He didn't need to; with infidelity and murder at its center, the case was already juicy.

What the assistant district attorney lacked in charisma, Mark Bellows made up for in spades. He was dressed and coiffed impeccably, but still managed to relate to the jury like he was an old best friend from high school. He spoke to the jurors personally, making sure to include eye contact with each of them during his short summation.

"Joe Wentner is an innocent man," Mark began. "The Prosecution is either going to say Joe knew his wife was being unfaithful and couldn't take it any longer, or that he just found out about her infidelity and flipped out. It doesn't matter which of those scenarios they say caused Joe to murder Garryn Monteith, because both are wrong. Joe Wentner didn't kill anyone. Now, it may look like Joe had a motive for murder," Mark went folksy, "but so did a lot of other people, including the real murderer. Who really killed Garryn Monteith? That's what we're here to find out."

Greg, as one of the first officers on the scene, was the first witness called to testify. Syda may have hung on his every word, but Pat was distracted once she noticed Tim, a late arrival, seated across the aisle from her. They overacted and ignored one another too much. If Syda had been paying attention, they were so obvious she would have noticed.

Greg's testimony was detailed and boring, but didn't take long. The most interesting thing Greg had to say was that he discovered a number of tubes of Super Glue on the premises.

Mark rose for cross-examination. "Officer Gonzales, did you search the belongings of the class members?"

"I did," Greg responded tersely.

"Did any of the students have Super Glue in their possession?"

"All of the students were in possession of tubes of Super Glue."

"Thank you, Officer Gonzales. No further questions."

Greg returned to his seat, leaned down to collect his hat, and discreetly give Syda a quick peck on the cheek before he left the courtroom.

Tim was called next. Pat may have zoned out as Greg was asked questions, but she didn't as Tim spoke. He was good at delivering narrative without putting the jury to sleep. When the Prosecution concluded and Mark approached Tim, she couldn't help but compare the two men.

Mark was urbane. His tailored white shirt cuffs were exactly the length beyond his suit jacket that *GQ* proscribed. His hair, with its smattering of gray, had been cut by a good professional. His shoes were expensive Italian classics. He oozed sophistication and intelligence.

Tim was the boy next door. He was nice-looking and had ridiculously broad shoulders and strong hands, but if the two were cast for a Hollywood movie, Tim would have been the best friend, the one who didn't get the girl.

Syda brought Pat out of her reverie with a jab to the ribs. She whispered in her ear, "Ooh, you know how I feel about Tim, but your attorney is gorgeous." She shook her hand in front of her like a fan.

"Please tell us, Officer Lindsey," Mark crooned, "when you decided Joe Wentner was guilty and stopped considering other suspects?"

"It's not my job to decide guilt or innocence, Mr. Bellows, so I never do. I follow all leads and leave the determination of guilt or innocence to the jury."

Mark was smooth. Tim was his match. Pat was impressed. Central casting would have been, as well.

When his testimony had been given, like Greg, Tim returned to his seat for his hat. He tucked it under his arm and marched, eyes straight ahead, past Syda and Pat without any sign of recognition.

The afternoon testimony was devoted to the county coroner's findings. He probably would have figured it out himself, but Pat was thrilled that she was the first to figure out how enough cyanide gas got into Garryn Monteith to kill him. She felt clever for having come up with the idea, even if the Coroner didn't give her credit for it.

If Garryn Monteith had ingested a lethal dose of cyanide, it would have been impossible to argue anyone except Joe had given it to him. But inhaled cyanide as the cause of death helped Joe's defense.

Mark concluded his cross-examination by asking the coroner a pertinent question. "Coroner Bates, if Super Glue tubes were the method used to introduce inhaled cyanide into Garryn Monteith's system, and all the participants in the Glass House class had them with them as part of their work kits, couldn't any one of them have poisoned the murder victim?"

"That's a reasonable assumption," the coroner answered.

On redirect, the Prosecution limited the list of potential killers by asking who among the class members would have had the knowledge about placement of the tubes within the kiln, timing for opening the kiln to place the tubes, and access to the kiln during that limited time window. The coroner acknowledged not all would have, but by the time the coroner had finished testifying, Mark had succeeded in planting his first tiny seed of doubt that Joe was the only one capable of killing Garryn Monteith.

On redirect, Mark threw in one other question for the

jury to think about overnight.

"Coroner Bates, is it correct that a lethal amount of cyanide would only be delivered to the first person who opened the kiln?"

"Yes, it is. The remaining cyanide would dissipate before other people in the room would be harmed by it."

"So if Joe Wentner killed Garryn Monteith because he was jealous of him, as the Prosecution suggests, we all must agree that Joe Wentner didn't want to harm his wife. If that's true, how could he take the chance that she wouldn't be the first one to open the kiln and inhale a lethal dose of cyanide?"

Pat knew the answer to that question because Lillian had told her: Garryn Monteith always insisted on opening the kiln on the last day of class. She knew, but the jury didn't. And she wondered if the Prosecution did, either, or if that bit of incriminating testimony was only in her head.

The Prosecution objected, saying the question called for speculation on the coroner's part; but Mark had done his job well, Pat acknowledged, and the best parts of the trial hadn't even started yet.

❊❊❊❊❊❊❊❊❊❊

Pat and Syda slipped into court the next day as Judge Blaine was rapping the courtroom to silence and sat near the back of the room, this time on the Defense side. Lillian Wentner was seated in the front row behind her husband, the unofficial site of all loyal wives. Pat noticed Suzanne

Cummings and Kandi Crusher near the front of the room together with another woman she recognized from class: Roberta Grumm. She knew all three had damaging things to say about Joe Wentner.

The Prosecution called Suzanne Cummings to the stand.

"Have you attended several classes at the Glass House over a period of years?"

"Yes."

"Were you aware that the defendant's wife, Lillian Wentner, and the murder victim, Garryn Monteith..."

Mark Bellows was on his feet interrupting the assistant district attorney before he finished his question.

"Your honor, the Defense stipulates to the fact that Lillian Wentner and Garryn Monteith had a long-term, occasional intimate relationship."

Pat heard a muted inhalation of breath in the courtroom.

Mark's interruption had not only startled the courtroom; it threw Robert Smith off his rhythm. The assistant district attorney fumbled through a few more questions that didn't add to his argument and then turned Suzanne Cummings over to Mark Bellows.

"No questions at this time, Your Honor."

Syda whispered in Pat's ear, "What's he up to?"

"I have no idea," Pat whispered back.

The Prosecution called Kandi Crusher.

"Mrs. Crusher, were you the sister of Peter Frieberg?'

"Half-sister, yes."

"Was your brother involved in a business relationship with the deceased, Garryn Monteith?"

"Yes, he was."

"Were they still in business at the time of your brother's death?"

"No. Their business dealings ended years ago."

"During the time your half-brother and Mr. Monteith were in business together, did your brother tell you that he was aware of a long-term relationship between the wife of the defendant and Mr. Monteith, one that continued after her marriage to Joe Wentner?"

Mark rose again. Pat expected him to proclaim whatever Kandi said about conversations with her brother would be hearsay. Instead he said, "Your honor we have already stipulated to that fact."

Once again the courtroom was left with nothing but the assistant district attorney's, "Nothing more, Your Honor," and Mark's, "No questions at this time, Your Honor."

"The Prosecution calls Roberta Grumm, Your Honor."

Roberta marched to the stand and raised her right hand even before she was asked to do so. She was dressed in a tailored suit and wore sensible shoes. She wore glasses, too, but they weren't thicker than the glasses worn by the assistant district attorney and several members of the jury.

"Mrs. Grumm…"

"Ms. Grumm."

"Ms. Grumm, did you see Lillian Wentner and her husband Joe Wentner in Carmel a few days before the class at which Garryn Monteith was murdered began?"

"I did."

"Did you speak to them?"

"No."

"Did you hear the conversation they were having?"

"I did."

The Prosecution must have coached Roberta Grumm on how to answer the question, Pat thought, since she didn't ramble or go off track on the stand like she had on the phone with her.

"Could you tell the Court what they said?"

"They were arguing, and Joe Wentner said he'd 'had it and wasn't going to put up with it anymore.' Lillian Wentner said he wouldn't have to because she wanted a divorce."

"Are you absolutely certain the couple you heard were Lillian and Joe Wentner?"

"Yes, I am."

"Why is that?"

"Because I recognized them when I came to the class at their studio."

Pat waited eagerly for Mark to start his cross-examination. Roberta Grumm's last statement wasn't exactly true and he knew it. Surely if he caught her in even a slight misstatement, he could weaken her testimony.

Instead of impugning her, however, Mark stated once again that the Defense had no questions at the present time. Why hadn't he tried to impeach her testimony?

"I'll meet you outside, Syda," Pat said when the lunch break came. "I want to talk to Mark."

She walked toward the Defense table, dodging the rest of the courtroom observers and witnesses headed in the other direction. The reaction she received from the three morning's witnesses as she passed them was varied. Roberta gave her a big smile, Kandi's reaction was friendly but subdued, and Suzanne's was indignant. She blocked Pat's way.

"What's wrong with that defense attorney?" she demanded. "Joe's not guilty. Why doesn't he defend him?"

"That's what I'm going to ask him. Excuse me, Suzanne."

The courtroom was almost empty by the time she reached Mark Bellows at the Defense table. He was seated, reviewing notes before putting them into his briefcase.

"Mark?"

He spun in his seat to greet her, flashing one of his perfect smiles. "Pat, hi. I noticed you've been in the courtroom from the beginning, but I don't think the Prosecution is going to call you after all, so you can head out until tomorrow—not that I want to chase you away; I enjoy seeing your pretty face. You'll be my last witness."

"I have been here from the beginning, and I've been watching and getting worried. You do have a plan to save Joe, don't you?"

He laughed out loud. "Of course I do."

"Why aren't you questioning witnesses?"

"Trust me. You'll see."

He rose and snapped his briefcase closed. "I'd invite you to lunch, but it would be unseemly to be seen with a witness, so dinner as soon as the trial is over?"

He didn't wait for her answer. Instead he strolled down

the aisle and out of the courtroom.

The afternoon session was technical and after two more hours, the Prosecution rested.

"The hour is late enough that we'll call it a day," the judge said. "We'll hear from the Defense beginning at 8:30 tomorrow morning."

"I've been told to be in court tomorrow for some possible redirect. Will that bother you?" Tim asked as he and Pat sipped wine after a quiet dinner at her house.

"I'll be fine as long as you don't sit near me and don't look at me. I find you quite distracting," Pat giggled.

"I'll sit in the last row and wear a bushy beard."

"That should work."

Tim took a long sip of wine and grew serious. "Not that I'm counting, but I think this is our ninth or tenth date. I'm tired of hiding us from Syda and Greg. I want to keep seeing you, maybe for the rest of my life. Is that okay with you?"

"More than okay. And if you don't mind, I want to exercise my woman's prerogative tonight."

※※※※※※※※※※

Pat couldn't get Syda to give court one more day, even though she promised day three might be exciting.

"I have all the material I need to write a court scene, and sitting there until my bum gets numb and my brain goes dead isn't like watching something dramatic on TV. Unless you need me there for moral support, I'll stick with Judge Judy from here on out.

"No, I'll be fine without you," Pat promised.

Mark wasted no time once Judge Blaine called the Court to order. "The Defense calls Angela Grinardi," he said in a crisp tone of voice.

Angela was seated in the last row, the place where Pat was trying not to look because she knew Tim would be there, and she hadn't noticed her when she came in.

Angela looked distressed as she was sworn in. Jet lag— Pat wondered—or something more?

"Mrs. Grinardi, I have just a few questions for you and then I'll let you fly back home to Maryland," Mark said in his most charming and friendly manner. "You were present when Garryn Monteith was murdered, weren't you?"

"Yes, I was."

"Was this the first time you took a class Mr. Monteith taught?"

"Yes, it was."

"Did you know Mr. Monteith prior to attending his class?"

"Yes, I did."

"Could you tell the Court how you knew him?"

Angela pulled herself up straighter in the witness seat than seemed possible. She hesitated for a few seconds before answering, weighing her words.

"He stole a patent from my late husband."

"Were you angry with the deceased because of that?"

Angela's eyes narrowed. "Of course I was."

"Mrs. Grinardi, did you have Super Glue with you for the class?"

"Yes."

"Were you aware that Super Glue contains cyanide?"

"It has a warning label saying it does, so yes, I was."

"Thank you, Mrs. Grinardi. No further questions." Mark nodded to the jury before he nodded to Judge Blaine.

The assistant district attorney asked Angela only one question: "Did you use Super Glue to kill Garryn Monteith?"

"I did not," she replied decisively.

"The Defense calls Kandi Crusher."

Kandi held her head high as she was reminded she was still under oath.

Mark Bellows asked her the same first four questions he asked Angela Grinardi and then settled back to let her answer how she knew Garryn Monteith. Her answer was as insolent as Angela Grinardi's had been.

"I knew him because of my brother. Garryn Monteith swindled him out of a great sum of money."

"Your brother, Mrs. Crusher, did he tell you about the lethality of Super Glue, or did you figure that out yourself?"

Assistant District Attorney Smith was on his feet with an objection, which the judge upheld. Judge Blaine instructed the jury to disregard Mark's question. Mark didn't need the jury to hear Kandi's answer. Juries could be told to disregard a question, but they never did.

"Thank you, Mrs. Crusher. No further questions at this time, but we reserve the right to recall the witness, Your Honor."

"So noted," Judge Blaine replied.

"The Defense calls Suzanne Cummings."

Pat felt as much anguish at what was about to befall Suzanne as the woman must have felt herself. Suzanne approached the witness stand like Anne Boleyn on her way to her beheading.

Mark began his questions as he had with the other women, but by the time he asked, "Was this the first class you took from Garryn Monteith?" everything changed.

"No."

"Miss Cummings, could you speak more loudly, please," the judge requested.

Suzanne cleared her throat. "No," she repeated.

"Approximately how many classes did you take from Mr. Monteith?"

"I don't know exactly."

"More than ten?"

"Yes."

"More than fifteen?"

"Yes," Suzanne's voice began to fade again.

Mark chocked his head, "More than twenty?"

"Probably."

"More than—"

The assistant district attorney was on his feet with another objection.

"Question withdrawn, Your Honor. I'm sure the jury

understands my point. It's safe to say Miss Cummings was a regular in Garryn Monteith's classes."

Mark paused and held up a finger as if what he asked next had just occurred to him. "Did you take glass-related classes from other instructors, as well?"

"No."

Suzanne was admonished again to speak up.

"No."

"Miss Cummings, in the many classes you took from Garryn Monteith, did you learn how firing in a kiln works?"

"Yes."

"Would you say you have knowledge of when a kiln might be opened early in the firing program without causing damage to the process?"

"Yes, I guess I would."

"Miss Cummings, did you ever have an intimate relationship with Garryn Monteith?"

Color rose in Suzanne's face.

"A long time ago."

"Miss Cummings, did you threaten any women in the classes that you attended?"

"On occasion." She thrust out her chest and spoke so loudly, everyone could hear her easily. "But I never hurt anyone, if that's what you're going to ask me next. I only sent letters and did little things. I never hurt anyone. And I only did things to women if they led Garryn on. He was a flirt; everyone knew he was—I didn't care—but I only did things if they flirted back. Some of them slept with him. I know they did. They deserved having little things done to them."

Pat understood what Mark was doing and understood he had to defend his client in any way he could. She didn't have to like watching it, though.

"Thank you, Miss Cummings. I think we've heard enough."

"Don't you want to hear about Lillian Wentner and what she did?" Suzanne shouted.

Mark smiled slyly. Assistant District Attorney Smith was apoplectic. "Your Honor," he pleaded.

"Since the witness opened that door, Your Honor," Mark stated calmly, "yes, Miss Cummings, I would."

"Objection," Robert Smith tried once again.

"I'll allow," Judge Blaine replied.

"Garryn and Lillian had been having an affair for a long time, every time he taught at the Glass House. I heard Lillian tell Garryn that she was going to leave her husband and go back to New York with him. But Garryn didn't want her to. He broke it off. He told her he just used her for 'booty calls.' That's what he said. Lillian went crazy. Ask her if she had Super Glue. Ask her if she knew when to open the kiln to put it in. Ask her!"

"Thank you, Miss Cummings."

"I think we need a break before the Prosecution questions Miss Cummings," the judge said.

"The Defense wishes to recall Kandi Crusher." Mark was back in crisp mode.

"Mrs. Crusher, would you tell the Court about the exchange you heard between Lillian Wentner and Garryn Monteith after the first day of class?"

"I returned to the studio after class because I forgot my purse. I heard them in the alcove part of the studio. They were fighting. Lillian told Garryn she was going to leave her husband so she could go back to New York with him. Garryn said he didn't want her to. He did say what Suzanne Cummings said he said. He told her she had been a 'lucrative booty call' but that he wouldn't be teaching any more classes at the Glass House."

"What was Lillian Wentner's reaction to what he said?"

"She screamed at him and sounded furious."

"Was she angry enough to kill him?"

"Calls for speculation, Your Honor," Assistant District Attorney Smith protested.

"I'll withdraw the question, Your Honor. Thank you, Mrs. Crusher, no further questions. At this time the Defense calls Pat Pirard."

As she was being sworn in, Pat glanced toward the back of the courtroom. Tim was in the last row. He was not wearing a bushy beard. She maintained the solemnity befitting the situation with great difficulty; after last night she desperately wanted to smile at him.

Pat's testimony began with a surprise. Mark made sure no one could see him do it, and then he winked at her.

"Ms. Pirard, you were hired by my firm to do research for this trial, were you not?"

"I was, at least for a while before I was terminated."

If she could have kicked herself, she would have. She knew the drill: witnesses needed to answer the question posed and then stop talking.

Mark didn't react. "During your time of employment, did you discover that about one in four women in the class had some connection with Garryn Monteith that might have caused them to, at the very least, dislike the man?"

"Objection."

"Overruled. You may answer the question, Ms. Pirard," Judge Blaine instructed.

"Yes."

"Have you been in the courtroom since jury selection?"

"Yes."

"And during that time, did you hear the testimony of Roberta Grumm, Angela Grinardi, Kandi Crusher, and Suzanne Cummings?"

"Yes, I did."

"Did you have conversations with those witnesses during the course of your investigation in which they told you the same things they testified to in court today?"

"Yes, I did."

"Did you also have a conversation with Lillian Wentner while no longer in my office's employ in which she told you details about her and Joe Wentner's marriage?"

"Yes."

"What did Lillian Wentner say about her husband's knowledge, or lack of knowledge, about her relationship with Garryn Monteith?"

"She said he knew about it all along."

"What did she say about the nature of their fidelity within their marriage?"

"She said her husband knew about her relationship with Garryn Monteith and accepted it because they had an open marriage."

There was so much noise in the courtroom that Pat felt like she had thrown a hand grenade among the spectators and jury.

"Did you tell her she had been overheard asking Joe for a divorce?"

"Yes."

"What did she say to you in regard to that?"

"She said that divorce was an idle threat which they sometimes directed at one another, but that they were still married after eighteen years."

"Thank you, Ms. Pirard. No further…well just one more question. You were present for the class Garryn Monteith taught at the Glass House, weren't you?"

"Yes, I took the class."

"Officer Tim Lindsey, as lead investigator, stated it is the conclusion of the investigation that the tubes of Super Glue which killed Garryn Monteith were introduced in the kiln during the preceding day's lunch break. Do you recall where Angela Grinardi, Kandi Crusher, Suzanne Cummings, and Lillian Wentner were during lunch that day?"

"Let me think," Pat faltered. "I spoke with Kandi Crusher for some of the lunch break…"

"But not all of it?"

"No, not all of it. I think Suzanne Cummings was in the bathroom. She usually spent breaks in there."

"Did you see her enter or leave the bathroom?"

"No. I just assumed that's where she was. I'm sorry. I don't remember where Angela Grinardi or Lillian Wentner were."

"And what about Joe Wentner? Do you remember where he was?"

"I do," Pat said brightly. "He was serving lunch. I spoke with him for a long time."

"Thank you. Now, no further questions, Your Honor."

Assistant District Attorney Smith spoke next. "Ms. Pirard, you seem to have a very good and very detailed memory of many conversations and observations you made during the class you took. You must remember, then, did you speak with Joe Wentner for the entire lunch break?

"No, not all of it."

"So it is possible he could have slipped out to the studio—"

"Objection, Your Honor. Calls for speculation."

Pat thought Assistant District Attorney Smith had just scored a win for the Prosecution.

"What did Joe Wentner have to say about Garryn Monteith?"

"Well, he said Garryn was a fussy eater and demanded gluten-free food." There was an undercurrent of chuckling in the courtroom. "Joe wasn't very happy that Garryn Monteith didn't want to eat the special breakfast rolls he made for him on the morning of the murder and insisted that he at least taste them. That's all I remember about his interaction with Garryn Monteith."

The assistant district attorney seemed disappointed as he said, "No further questions, Your Honor."

Pat was leaving the witness stand when Mark Bellows announced, "The Defense rests, Your Honor."

"On that note we'll take a lunch break," Judge Blaine said. "Eat hardy, members of the jury, because this afternoon you'll start deliberating on the guilt or innocence of Joe Wentner."

Pat's eyes searched the courtroom for Tim. She felt shaky and wished he was there to hug her, but he had already left.

Summations began in the afternoon session with the Prosecution going first. Assistant District Attorney Smith reminded the jury that Joe had means and opportunity to kill Garryn Monteith, and that his motive was jealousy.

"Lillian Wentner asked her husband for a divorce so she could run away with the murder victim. Joe Wentner may have tolerated his wife's infidelity for years, but that was the final straw. He wasn't about to let her leave him for her long-time lover."

The Prosecution's summation was concise and damaging. Then it was Mark Bellows's turn to speak.

"I expect some of you wanted to hear Joe Wentner stand before you and insist he is a wrongly accused man. He could have told you he is innocent, but there is no need for him to do so. The facts prove that he is. Joe knew of

Garryn Monteith's relationship for all of his marriage. He accepted it. You heard testimony that Lillian Wentner asked him for a divorce and planned to leave him. But you also heard it was a threat she made frequently.

"Most importantly, you heard from multiple witnesses that Garryn Monteith ended his relationship with Lillian Wentner the day before his murder and that she was furious about that.

"Joe Wentner may have had the opportunity and means to put lethal cyanide tubes in the kiln, but so did other people who also had motive—possibly more motive than Joe Wentner did—for killing Garryn Monteith.

"Angela Grinardi's husband had a valuable patent stolen by the murder victim. Mrs. Grinardi is widowed and struggling to put her children through college. How different might her situation be if Garryn Monteith wasn't a thief? Enough motive for murder?" Mark shrugged dramatically.

"Kandi Crusher's brother was another of Garryn Monteith's victims. Did she hate the murdered man enough to avenge her brother's mistreatment?" Mark shrugged again.

"Then there's Suzanne Cummings. She clearly stalked Garryn Monteith for years. She resented the other women he 'flirted with.' You have to wonder if she finally reached the breaking point and decided to direct her rage at him instead of them.

"Miss Cummings asked a good question during her testimony: 'What about Lillian Wentner?' We know she told Garryn Monteith she was leaving her husband so she could be with him. What was his reaction to her profession of love? He said he didn't want her, that she was nothing more to him than a lucrative booty call. All those years, an offer to end her marriage to a stand-up guy, and all for what? A smack-down by the man she was doing it all for. Do you think she had a good motive for murder?

"Joe Wentner pleaded not guilty. We don't have to prove his innocence, ladies and gentlemen of the jury. You don't have to be one hundred percent sure he is innocent to acquit him, either. If you think Joe Wentner might have murdered Garryn Monteith, do you have any doubts about your conclusion? Can you be certain beyond a reasonable doubt that Joe Wentner killed Mr. Monteith, or is the field too crowded with other people who also had the means, opportunity, and a motive to wish Garryn Monteith dead? Remember, to convict Joe Wentner, you must be certain of his guilt beyond a reasonable doubt. Beyond a reasonable doubt," Mark repeated, emphasizing each word.

"Are you sure, ladies and gentlemen of the jury? Because if you have any reasonable doubt about Joe Wentner, you must acquit him on the count of murder in the first degree."

Mark Bellows had mesmerized the jury with reasonable doubt. They returned a not-guilty verdict in time for everyone to go home for dinner.

17

Pat lingered after the verdict was read and so did Tim and Greg, who had returned to the courtroom when word got out that the jury had concluded their work. She greeted them with a nod and a formal, "Officers."

"What happens next?" she asked.

"We're not sure, Pat," Greg answered. "Joe Wentner's off the hook, that's clear. The DA will have to decide if charges will be brought against anyone else."

"We're all still a little in shock, ma'am," Tim replied, working on his professional distance. "We thought the assistant DA made a strong case."

"He did—just not as strong as my case," Mark Bellows said as he reached the group with Lillian and Joe in tow. He grabbed Pat's hand and pulled her toward him, lifted her off her feet, and spun her around in wild celebration before he planted a kiss on her lips.

Pat was so surprised, she didn't protest. Tim looked at her quizzically, one eyebrow so high it almost reached his hairline.

"Come on, Pat," Mark said. "We're having dinner to celebrate. You were a huge part of our success, so you're coming with us. Sorry, officers, you're not invited," he laughed.

She was dragged off with the newly victorious, able only to look at Tim briefly over her shoulder before she was pulled from the courtroom.

They went to Oswald's, a favorite of Mark's, Pat surmised.

"Order the most expensive things on the menu," Mark said jovially, still higher on an adrenalin rush than either of the Wentners. "We'll put it on Joe's defense bill. And we need champagne."

Pat was the only one at the table who wasn't celebrating. She always believed Joe was innocent, but now she wondered about Lillian and stared at her hard, trying to see if she was looking at a murderess seated across the table from her.

Mark cajoled, "Please don't feel like you were used, Pat, although you were a little, but for a good cause. I had to let you think the reasonable doubt defense I planned wasn't a strong one so you'd keep pushing as hard as you could to find evidence I could use."

"I thought you knew me better than to think I needed pushing to do my best?" Pat replied coolly.

"I do, but like you said, you were new to the job and untried. I also needed your testimony. I told you you'd make a good witness. Someone had to tie all the women's declarations together on the stand. You were perfect in that role.

"I figured you might take what I just said like you did,

but I'll make it up to you, I promise," Mark flashed her an exceptionally warm smile.

"I can't thank you enough for what you did," Joe said.

"My pleasure, Joe. I always knew you were innocent."

As Pat proclaimed Joe's innocence, she noticed Lillian stare at her husband. An odd look fleetingly crossed her face and she pressed her lips together hard.

"Well, cheers," Lillian said hesitantly and raised her champagne glass. She turned her eyes toward Pat as they all sipped their wine.

Pat wasn't sure what she was reading in Lillian's expression, but it disturbed her. Lillian was guarding a secret of some sort: was it guilt or something else?

"So, Mark," Pat queried, "Joe's cleared, but you presented a pretty credible case that Lillian murdered Garryn." She watched Lillian closely as she asked, "What happens if the DA charges her?"

Mark smiled broadly. "It's always a gamble when you go to trial, but I have a plan, should that happen. Everything hinged on keeping both Lillian and Joe off the witness stand. The prosecution couldn't compel the defendant to testify in a criminal case, so that part was easy. Stipulating to Lillian's affair with Monteith made her a useless witness to them. If they asked her anything about Joe's knowledge or frame of mind, I would have shut them down with objections of speculation or privileged conversation between a husband and wife. Lillian couldn't be compelled to testify against her husband.

"And now, because neither gave testimony under oath,

the prosecution can't so much as charge either with perjury for what they say if there's a future trial. If Lillian goes to trial, both Lillian and Joe can testify in her defense and, if we need to, we can aim guilt back at Joe, who can't be charged again because of double jeopardy."

"Whew, plan or not, that still sounds dangerous," Pat said.

Lillian spoke up. "I accepted the risk freely." Then she spoke to Joe intimately, as if Pat and Mark weren't sharing a table with them. "I haven't been the best wife, certainly," she said to her husband, "but you stood by me. I love you, I really do. After what you did because of me, I'm just grateful I had a chance to protect you. I'll be a better wife in the future, I promise."

"Lillian?" Joe's face contorted into a look of horror, "Do you think I killed Garryn?"

"You did, didn't you? To save our marriage, to save us?"

"No!" he exclaimed. "No, I didn't."

"If not you, my love, then who? All those other women had grudges against Garryn, but none of them had reason enough to go so far as to kill him. That's right, isn't it Mark? Pat?"

All eyes were on Lillian.

"You all think I did it?" she asked suddenly when she realized why. "Pat, no, I led you on so you could testify against me at Joe's trial. My 'slip of the tongue' at your house, it was all part of the plan. Tell them, Mark!"

Mark remained silent for several seconds. Finally, he

said, "The breakup testimony Kandi Crusher and Suzanne Cummings gave was pretty damning."

Joe took her hand. "It's okay, Lillian, sweetheart. I'll say I killed him. You won't be convicted."

"I better not be. I didn't kill him!"

Lillian pushed her chair back from the table as tears started down her cheeks. "I didn't kill him; how could you all think I did?" she asked softly before she ran from the restaurant.

"My wife needs me, and I need to apologize for thinking what I did," Joe said as he got to his feet and followed Lillian.

"Mark, I'm going, too," Pat said.

"No, stay and have dinner with me. You know I've wanted us to get closer for quite some time. Now we have a chance to."

Pat smiled at him sympathetically. "Do you know the Shakespeare quote about the tides of men?"

"Sort of."

"It has to do with missed opportunity. I'm afraid our opportunity has passed, Mark. Sorry." She shouldered her purse and got up. "Enjoy your dinner," she said, and left him sitting alone.

As soon as she got outside of the restaurant, Pat called Tim.

"Are you free for Thai takeout?" she asked.

"I thought you were having dinner with your attorney boyfriend." She could hear the hurt in his voice.

"There's been a change of plans. And where did you get

the idea Mark Bellows was more than my employer?"

"Greg told me. He said you told Syda you had a thing for the clever Mr. Bellows. Besides, I saw the way he kissed you."

"Are you jealous?" Pat asked in amazement.

"Of course I'm jealous. The way I feel about you, the thought of sharing you with anyone else...I'm not like Joe Wentner. It's not something I can do."

"I never thought we'd be having a commitment talk on the phone—that seems like something we should do cuddled together—but I can't let you wonder about me. I can't hurt you like that, not even for an hour, especially after what I witnessed tonight.

"Greg got his timeline wrong. '*Had* a thing for him' is the operative phase. I kind of had an unrequited crush on Mark Bellows, but it was before us. And about that kiss you saw: if you'd been looking at it impartially with your lead investigator eyes, you would have noticed he kissed me, but I didn't kiss him back."

"I'm way beyond looking at you impartially," Tim said. "You know that. Okay. I'll pick up Thai and be at your house in forty-five."

"Tim, when you get here, park in my driveway. Please, no more sneaking around and hiding. I want to let everyone in the world know how I feel about you."

Even with Tim next to her, Pat couldn't sleep. She had too much on her mind. She slipped out of bed, careful not to wake Dot, who was asleep in her dog bed a few feet from her, and tiptoed to the living room.

Over their Thai takeout she and Tim had had their first serious talk about the future. They agreed that, after ten dates, they still liked each other. She should have felt pure joy imagining how one day they would probably tell each other I love you—it felt like that talk was coming, too. But she'd reached thirty-five and not just mouthed the words "I'm a strong, independent woman" because they were vogueish. She was strong and independent: in charge of her own destiny. Tim was no little rebound romance. If she allowed herself to fall in love with him, he'd have the power to hurt her. That part of love scared her.

The aborted dinner with Lillian and Joe hadn't helped. Their story was like O. Henry's *The Gift of the Magi* reimagined as a nightmarish tale. Lillian thought Joe had killed Garryn Monteith to save their marriage. She let Mark Bellows make her a prime suspect to save her husband from conviction. Joe believed Lillian killed Garryn and he was prepared to die in jail to protect her. How could two people be in love and yet get everything about one another so wrong?

Wimsey's yowl broke her reverie.

"I'm sorry," she could hear Tim say from her bedroom. He backed into the living room with his hands in the air in a gesture of apology. "I'm sorry," he repeated, half to Wimsey and half to her.

He sat down on the sofa next to her. "I tripped on your cat. I don't think he liked me before, now he's going to hate me."

"He likes you well enough, he's just not demonstrative." Pat giggled. "You're going to have to learn the sleeping arrangements around here, though, because he only has so much patience with humans."

"Why are you out here alone instead of with me, keeping me safe by giving me navigation directions?" he asked.

"I couldn't sleep. I was thinking about Lillian and Joe and the trial and," she was determined their communication was never going to be secretive and presumptive like Lillian and Joe's must have become. She told him the truth, "and us, too. It's funny how frightened I get thinking about commitment and how sure I am about it as soon as I'm near you."

"Then stay close to me," he said gently. "The sun's not near to rising; should we go back to bed?"

"You can, but I can't sleep. I keep thinking about what happens next, not with us, with the murder. Do you think the DA will charge Lillian?"

Tim yawned and scratched his ear. "My bet is he won't. As guilty as she seemed in the skilled hands of Mr. Bellows, when he's representing her, he's going to turn things around and make Joe look guilty and cause just as much uncertainty in the jury's mind as he did in Wentner's trial. He'll drag in all the other suspects, too, to really muddy the water. Trials are expensive, and I don't think the DA will spend money on what has more than a fifty-fifty chance of being a losing proposition."

Pat frowned.

"You said you didn't think she did it anyway, didn't you?" he asked.

"Yeah," Pat sighed. "I was so sure she killed Garryn Monteith for all the reasons that came up at trial, but after tonight, no, I don't think she did. Her denial was completely believable and her reaction when she realized Joe thought she was a murderer, well, it was heartbreaking. I think her astonishment was genuine."

"If not either of the Wentners, then who?" Tim asked.

"That's the question keeping me up."

"Are you sure no one else besides the women you found in the class had a reason to kill Monteith?"

"I did careful and thorough research. I'm sure there were no hidden grudges among the class."

"Then it has to be one of your other three suspects."

Pat nodded. "Will the DA try charging one of them?"

"I've been in charge of this investigation so I've seen everything we have about all three women, including what you gave me," Tim said as he smiled and leaned toward her to kiss her forehead. "Your investigation on them was painstaking; we don't have anything more.

"If you look at them," he continued, "Mrs. Grinardi may have been planning to settle an old score in her own way, but what Monteith did to her husband, stealing his patent…that was so long ago and, yes, I know murderers think they're going to get away with it and all that, but it's hard to imagine a woman who knows her children will suffer if she gets caught, who's never committed any kind of crime in her life, killing someone over a long-ago patent theft.

"The other reason I don't like her for murder is that she doesn't seem like someone who might risk hurting anyone else. Lillian opened the kiln on the first day; why wouldn't Mrs. Grinardi have thought she'd do that the second day? She had no reason to harm Lillian, I don't think she'd take the chance."

"I think you're right," Pat agreed. "It's such a long road between shaming and embarrassing someone and killing them, and I don't think she went down it."

"You could say the same thing about your game-named woman," Tim offered. "Long-time-ago grudge, no history of criminal activity, and no reason to risk hurting Lillian Wentner.

"Now you've got me thinking about this just like you are. We're not going back to bed, are we?" Tim asked.

"No, we're not. I better make us some coffee."

Tim followed Pat to the kitchen. "That leaves the weird little mouse."

"Weird little mouse? Is that what the Sherriff's Department calls Suzanne Cummings?"

Tim laughed, "Yes, but if you ever let it slip that I told you, I'll deny all knowledge of private moments with you and say it must have been Greg who told you about that tag. Think how bad you'd feel getting your friend in trouble."

"Your department nicknaming is safe with me."

"I have a problem with the mouse, too. She's a stalker," Tim said, "we'll give her that…"

"And she has a history of acting out," Pat added.

"Yeah, but she's never attacked a person and her breaking the windshield of your car seems to have been as violent as she ever got. Then there's her long history of knowing about Lillian and Monteith. How many classes did you say she attended at the Glass House? She never so much as raised a finger against either of them before, and she had plenty of opportunity to. Why would she change her pattern now?"

"I don't know."

Pat inhaled sharply and dropped the open container of coffee she was holding on the floor, sending grounds everywhere. "Yes, I do! I've known why for weeks. Why didn't I see it before? Suzanne changed her pattern because it was over between Lillian and Garryn, and he wasn't coming back to her like she always thought he would when they broke up."

"What?"

"Oh, my golly, Tim, she did it. Don't you see? She overheard Garryn breaking it off with Lillian. He may have been planning to end their relationship even before Lillian offered to run away with him, and Suzanne may have guessed it. She said Garryn never carried on with anyone at Lillian's classes because he had Lillian there, but he flirted with me. When Suzanne admitted she broke my windshield, she said she did it not because she hated me, but because I was right."

"Right about what?"

"When I was trying to unsettle her, I told her he wasn't

interested in her anymore, which is why he tried to come on to me. It turns out that I was right.

"Tim, she took so many classes, she knew the drill. Lillian said she always acted like she was going to open the kiln on the last morning, but that Garryn always insisted on doing it. It was part of their performance. Suzanne knew Garryn would be the one to open the kiln."

"But she never did anything to him," Tim said. "She only went after the women he was interested in. You said she loved Monteith and would never hurt him."

"I must have been wrong about that. Or, umm, maybe not exactly..." Pat stopped speaking.

"The case isn't closed. I can bring her in for questioning in the morning without ruffling any feathers."

"I need to talk to her. Is there any way I can sit in when she's being questioned?"

"Not unless you're with her lawyer."

Pat's first call in the morning was to Mark Bellows. Her words were terse and concise. "Mark, you have to rehire me for ten minutes. Suzanne Cummings is being brought in for questioning this morning. You have to get her to hire you, and I have to come with you when you meet with her."

"What's going on, Pat? How do you know this?"

"You owe me. No questions; just do it."

Mark called her back about an hour later. "They're holding Suzanne Cummings for questioning at the main jail on Water Street. I'm on my way there."

Pat beat him to the main jail by a few seconds.

"Mark Bellows, counsel representing Suzanne Cummings," he said when he was asked to identify himself, "and my associate, Pat Pirard."

They were shown to an interview room where a pale Suzanne sat. When she saw Pat, she jumped up and held out her arms.

"Pat, they think I killed Garryn," she said, her voice filled with so much emotion and trembling, she was hard to understand.

Pat hugged her and then put her arm around the stricken woman's shoulder and helped her back into her seat. Pat sat down next to her and kept her arm around her as she took Suzanne's hand in hers.

"You did, Suzanne, didn't you?" Pat asked gently.

"No," she whimpered, "no I…"

"You didn't mean to, though, did you?" Pat comforted.

"No. Of course not. I've never hurt anyone and I would never hurt Garryn."

"What happened, Suzanne?"

Suzanne moaned. It took a minute before she spoke. "After he and Lillian had their fight, I followed him back to his hotel in Santa Cruz. I figured out which room he was staying in. When I knocked on his door, he let me in. He looked awful, poor man.

"I told him not to worry, that I would be there for him. He said not to bother—he was so kind in the way he said it, not at all like he had been when he broke it off with Lillian—because he was flying back to New York as soon as the class was over.

"I knew if he left, we'd never be together. I needed more time with him to make him realize he still loved me. So I decided to make him sick enough that he'd miss his flight. I thought I could take him home with me and nurse him back to health...I-I didn't know I put too many tubes of Super Glue in the kiln. I didn't mean to kill him. It was an accident; I loved him."

Suzanne leaned against Pat and convulsed in sobs.

"Mark will take good care of you. Everything will be all right."

As Pat was leaving, Suzanne called after her. "I never would have let them send Joe to jail. I swear. Please tell him I would have confessed if he had been convicted."

"I'll tell him, Suzanne."


Pat called Syda when she got home and told her about last night's dinner with Joe, Lillian, and Mark and about Suzanne's confession. She left out what happened during the rest of last night and the wee hours of the morning.

"What a story this would make for a book. We make such a great investigating team, I could be like Doctor Watson and write about our adventures. We'd be a modern-day female Doctor Watson and Sherlock Holmes."

"What happened to Rowdy Dick?"

"After he became Sam Sleuther, and then Sam Slugger, or Slaughter—I forget—I got bored with him."

Pat started to laugh, but was overtaken by a loud yawn.

"You sound like a wreck, BFF, but I know just what

you need."

"Some sleep?"

"That, too. But what you really need is a major distraction to take your mind off the whole Suzanne killing Garryn thing, not to mention the Wentners, or that gorgeous attorney things didn't work out with. How about you let me arrange that dinner with Tim and us that you promised you'd let me do?"

"That sounds like a great idea. How soon can we do it?"

"You're not going to try to wiggle out of it?" Syda said in disbelief. "In that case, tonight, before you have a change of heart."

"At this point I think it's too late for me to change my mind. My heart's pretty set, Syda. See you tonight."

"Oh, and remember to wear your green dress," Syda said quickly before they disconnected.

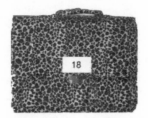

Did men get circles under their eyes from lack of sleep? Pat wondered about that as she tried to cover hers with a light touch of concealer. She'd know once she saw Tim. She took a look at herself in her long mirror. Syda was right about the green dress; circles or not, she looked good.

"I won't be too late, Dot, even if tonight is going to be a big one. See you later. Wimsey, you're in charge."

Pat parked her sunburst-yellow car behind Tim's Highlander in front of Syda and Greg's house and walked toward their front door with a huge smile on her face.

Greg answered the door and invited her inside. Syda was smiling, too. She looped her arm through Tim's and pulled him toward Pat.

"It's been a few weeks, but you remember my best friend Pat, don't you, Tim?"

He didn't have circles under his eyes.

Tim gave her a once-over worthy of Syda's original detective, Rowdy Dick.

"Wow!" he said enthusiastically.

He disentangled himself from Syda, slipped his arm

258

around Pat's waist, bent her backward, and kissed her.

"I certainly do," he said when she was upright again.

"What have you two been up to?" Greg managed to ask suspiciously. Syda had no words, not one.

Tim walked Pat to her car. "I need to go home and put together a go-bag," he said. "Is it okay if I bring it over tomorrow night?"

"I'll make some space in my bathroom and closet. Just a little bit at first, and then we'll see?"

"That's just what I had in mind."

Their goodnight kiss almost made them change their minds about going home in different directions. But they were now out in public; they could take their time and savor every moment getting to know one another as a couple. No need to rush.

Pat was tired when she got home. Yesterday was rough and, except for a brief nap, it had been almost twenty-four hours since she'd slept, even fitfully. Her office was dark, but the light on her answering device blinked red; she could see it on her way to her bedroom. Much as she knew she should ignore it, it wasn't in her nature to let anything like a blinking red light go until morning.

"Hey, Pat, it's Roger Drago. So I hear from Dick Drinker you're in the private investigating business. I went to a doozy of a funeral last week. This rich dame—she was a client of mine—croaked at the funeral."

Pat knew Roger Drago was originally from New Jersey,

and she could hear it in his voice; but she was never sure if his joy in sounding like a forties mobster was cultivated, or the way he spoke because of his upbringing.

"That was bad enough, but now it looks like she was murdered, and the police don't know who did it, and I don't know who gets her dough. Can you be a doll and help me out? Call me."

Pat fell asleep happy. There was Tim, of course, and watching Syda's reaction to their announcement that they were, as Syda said, "involved," and the sorting out of what had happened to Garryn Monteith and why. But it looked like she had another reason to be happy, too. It looked like PIP Inc. was about to become her next full-time gig.

## About the Author

Nancy Lynn Jarvis left the real estate profession after she started having so much fun writing the Regan McHenry Real Estate Mysteries series that she let her license lapse. She's enjoyed writing about Regan and her husband, Tom, but wanted to do something different for her next book.

PIP Inc. introduces a new protagonist and is the first book in a planned series featuring not-quite-licensed Private Investigator Pat Pirard.

After earning a BA in behavioral science from San Jose State University, Nancy worked in the advertising department of the *San Jose Mercury News*. A move to Santa Cruz meant a new job as a librarian and later a stint as the business manager for Shakespeare/Santa Cruz at UCSC.

Currently she's enjoying being a member of Mystery Writers of America, Sisters in Crime, and Santa Cruz Women of Mystery.

Nancy Lynn Jarvis

## Join the Team

For small presses, getting exposure in the marketplace dominated by big publishers is a challenge, but it is also one where you as a reader can help us enormously by spreading the word.

So, if you have enjoyed this book, please help us to promote it and other titles by Good Read Publishers and Good Read Mysteries.

There's a wide range of ways you can do so, including:

- Recommending the book to your friends
- Posting a review on Amazon or other book websites like Goodreads
- Reviewing it on your blog
- Tweeting about it and giving a link to our website at http://www.nancylynnjarvis.com
- Suggesting the book to your book club
- Posting a comment on your Facebook page
- Liking our Facebook page at Good Read Publishers
- Pinning it at Pinterest
- Anything else that you think of!

Many thanks for your help—it's much appreciated.

At http://www.nancylynnjarvis.com you can:

- Read the first chapters of the books in the Regan McHenry Mystery Series.

- Meet Mags and her group of octogenarian bank robbers.

- Have a look at *Cozy Food: 128 Cozy Mystery Writers Share Their Favorite Recipes* and *Santa Cruz Weird*, a short story anthology written about Santa Cruz County by local authors.

- Review reader comments and email your own.

- Ask Nancy questions about her books and the next book in the PIP Inc. series.

- Find out about upcoming events, book club discounts, and arrange for Nancy to talk to your book club or group.

Books are also available for your Kindle, iPad, and other e-readers including your smart phone at Amazon.com.

Made in the USA
Monee, IL
04 April 2021

63718750R00157